THE FRONTIER

MAURICE LEBLANC

THE FRONTIER

BY

MAURICE LEBLANC

AUTHOR OF " ARSENE LUPIN," "813," ETC.

TRANSLATED BY

ALEXANDER TEIXEIRA DE MATTOS

WILDSIDE PRESS

Published by
Wildside Press, LLC
P.O. Box 301
Holicong, PA 18928-0301 USA
www.wildsidepress.com

Wildside Press Edition: MMIII

CONTENTS

PART I

PART II

CONTENTS

PART III

THE FRONTIER

PART I

CHAPTER I

" THEY'VE done it ! "

" What ? "

" The German frontier-post . . . at the circus of the Butte-aux-Loups."

" What about it ? "

" Knocked down."

" Nonsense ! "

" See for yourself."

Old Morestal stepped aside. His wife came out of the drawing-room and went and stood by the telescope, on its tripod, at the end of the terrace.

" I can see nothing," she said, presently.

" Don't you see a tree standing out above the others, with lighter foliage ? "

" Yes."

" And, to the right of that tree, a little lower down, an empty space surrounded by fir-trees ? "

" Yes."

" That's the circus of the Butte-aux-Loups and it marks the frontier at that spot."

3

"Ah, I've got it! . . . There it is! . . . You mean on the ground, don't you? Lying flat on the grass, exactly as if it had been rooted up by last night's storm. . . ."

"What are you talking about? It has been fairly felled with an axe: you can see the gash from here."

"So I can . . . so I can. . . ."

She stood up and shook her head:

"That makes the third time this year. . . . It will mean more unpleasantness."

"Fiddle-de-dee!" he exclaimed. "All they've got to do is to put up a solid post, instead of their old bit of wood." And he added, in a tone of pride, "The French post, two yards off, doesn't budge, you know!"

"Well, of course not! It's made of cast-iron and cemented into the stone."

"Let them do as much then! It's not money they're wanting . . . when you think of the five thousand millions they robbed us of! . . . No, but, I say . . . three of them in eight months! . . . How will the people take it, on the other side of the Vosges?"

He could not hide the sort of gay and sarcastic feeling of content that filled his whole being and he walked up and down the terrace, stamping his feet as hard as he could on the ground.

But, suddenly going to his wife, he seized her by the arm and said, in a hollow voice:

"Would you like to know what I really think?"

"Yes."

"Well, all this will lead to trouble."

"No," said the old lady, quietly.

"How do you mean, no?"

"We've been married five-and-thirty years; and, for five-and-thirty years, you've told me, week after week, that we shall have trouble. So, you see. . . ."

She turned away from him and went back to the drawing-room again, where she began to dust the furniture with a feather-broom.

He shrugged his shoulders, as he followed her indoors:

"Oh, yes, you're the placid mother, of course! Nothing excites you. As long as your cupboards are tidy, your linen all complete and your jams potted, you don't care! . . . Still, you ought not to forget that they killed your poor father."

"I don't forget it . . . only, what's the good? It's more than forty years ago. . . ."

"It was yesterday," he said, sinking his voice, "yesterday, no longer ago than yesterday. . . ."

"Ah, there's the postman!" she said, hurrying to change the conversation.

She heard a heavy footstep outside the windows opening on the garden. There was a rap at the knocker on the front-door. A minute later, Victor, the man-servant, brought in the letters.

" Oh! " said Mme. Morestal. " A letter from the boy. . . . Open it, will you? I haven't my spectacles. . . . I expect it's to say that he will arrive this evening: he was to have left Paris this morning."

" Not at all! " cried M. Morestal, glancing over the letter. " Philippe and his wife have taken their two boys to some friends at Versailles and started with the intention of sleeping last night at the Ballon de Colnard, seeing the sunrise and doing the rest of the journey on foot, with their knapsacks on their backs. They will be here by twelve."

She at once lost her head:

" And the storm! What about last night's storm? "

" My son doesn't care about the storm! It won't be the first that the fellow's been through. It's eleven o'clock. He will be with us in an hour."

" But that will never do! There's nothing ready for them! "

She at once went to work, like the active little old woman that she was, a little too fat, a little tired, but wide-awake still and so methodical, so orderly in her ways that she never made a superfluous movement or one that was not calculated to bring her an immediate advantage.

As for him, he resumed his walk between the terrace and the drawing-room. He strode with long, even steps, holding his body erect, his chest flung out and his hands in the pockets of his jacket, a blue-drill gardening-jacket, with the point of a pruning-shears and the stem of a pipe sticking out of it. He was tall and broad-shouldered; and his fresh-coloured face seemed young still, in spite of the fringe of white beard in which it was framed.

"Ah," he exclaimed, "what a treat to set eyes upon our dear Philippe again! It must be three years since we saw him last. Yes, of course, not since his appointment as professor of history in Paris. By Jove, the chap has made his way in the world! What a time we shall give him during the fortnight that he's with us! Walking . . . exercise. . . . He's all for the open-air life, like old Morestal!"

He began to laugh:

"Shall I tell you what would be the thing for him? Six months in camp between this and Berlin!"

"I'm not afraid," she declared. "He's been through the Normal School. The professors keep to their garrisons in time of war."

"What nonsense are you talking now?"

" The school-master told me so."

He gave a start:

" What!   Do you mean to say you still speak to that dastard? "

" He's quite a decent man," she replied.

" He!   A decent man!   With theories like his! "

She hurried from the room, to escape the explosion.   But Morestal was fairly started:

" Yes, yes, theories!   I insist upon the word: theories!   As a district-councillor, as Mayor of Saint-Élophe, I have the right to be present at his lessons.   Oh, you have no idea of his way of teaching the history of France! . . . In my time, the heroes were the Chevalier d'Assas, Bayard, La Tour d'Auvergne, all those beggars who shed lustre on our country.   Nowadays, it's Mossieu Étienne Marcel, Mossieu Dolet. . . . Oh, a nice set of theories, theirs! "

He barred the way to his wife, as she entered the room again, and roared in her face:

" Do you know why Napoleon lost the battle of Waterloo? "

" I can't find that large breakfast-cup anywhere," said Mme. Morestal, engrossed in her occupation.

" Well, just ask your school-master; he'll give you the latest up-to-date theories about Napoleon."

" I put it down here, on this chest, with my own hand."

" But there, they're doing all they can to distort the children's minds."

" It spoils my set."

" Oh, I swear to you, in the old days, we'd have ducked our school-master in the horse-pond, if he had dared. . . . But, by Jove, France had a place of her own in the world then! And such a place!

. . . That was the time of Solferino! . . . Of Magenta! . . . We weren't satisfied with chucking down frontier-posts in those days: we crossed the frontiers . . . and at the double, believe me . . ."

He stopped, hesitating, pricking up his ears. Trumpet-blasts sounded in the distance, ringing from valley to valley, echoing and re-echoing against the obstacles formed by the great granite rocks and dying away to right and left, as though stifled by the shadow of the forests.

He whispered, excitedly:

" The French bugle. . . ."

" Are you sure? "

" Yes, there are troops of Alpines manœuvring . . . a company from Noirmont. . . . Listen . . . listen. . . . What gaiety! . . . What swagger! . . . I tell you, close to the frontier like this, it takes such an air. . . ."

She listened too, seized with the same excitement, and asked, anxiously:

"Do you really think that war is possible?"

"Yes," he replied, "I do."

They were silent for a moment. And Morestal continued:

"It's a presentiment with me. . . . We shall have it all over again, as in 1870. . . . And, mark you, I hope that this time . . ."

She put down her breakfast-cup, which she had found in a cupboard, and, leaning on her husband's arm:

"I say, the boy's coming . . . with his wife. She's a dear girl and we're very fond of her. . . . I want the house to look nice for them, bright and full of flowers. . . . Go and pick the best you have in your garden."

He smiled:

"That's another way of saying that I'm boring you, eh? I can't help it. I shall be just the same to my dying day. The wound is too deep ever to heal."

They looked at each other for a while with a great gentleness, like two old travelling-companions, who, from time to time, for no particular reason, stop, exchange glances or thoughts and then resume their journey.

He asked:

"Must I cut my roses? My Gloires de Dijon?"

" Yes."

" Come along then! I'll be a hero!"

* * *

Morestal, the son and grandson of well-to-do
farmers, had increased his fathers' fortune tenfold
by setting up a mechanical saw-yard at Saint-
Élophe, the big neighbouring village. He was a
plain, blunt man, as he himself used to say, " with
no false bottom, nothing in my hands, nothing up
my sleeves;" just a few moral ideas to guide his
course through life, ideas as old and simple as could
be. And those few ideas themselves were subject
to a principle that governed his whole existence and
ruled all his actions, the love of his country, which,
in Morestal, stood for regret for the past, hatred
of the present and, especially, the bitter recollection
of defeat.

Elected Mayor of Saint-Élophe and a district-
councillor, he sold his works and built, within view
of the frontier, on the site of a ruined mill, a large
house designed after his own plans and constructed,
so to speak, under his own eyes. The Morestals had
lived here for the last ten years, with their two
servants: Victor, a decent, stout, jolly-faced man,
and Catherine, a Breton woman who had nursed
Philippe as a baby.

They saw but few people, outside a small number of friends, of whom the most frequent visitors were the special commissary of the government, Jorancé, and his daughter Suzanne.

The Old Mill occupied the round summit of a hill with slopes shelving down in a series of fairly large gardens, which Morestal cultivated with genuine enthusiasm. The property was surrounded by a high wall, the top of which was finished off with an iron trellis bristling with spikes. A spring leapt from place to place and fell in cascades to the bottom of the rocks decked with wild flowers, moss, lichen and maiden-hair ferns.

Morestal picked a great armful of flowers, laid waste his rose-garden, sacrificed all the Gloires de Dijon of which he was so proud and returned to the drawing-room, where he himself arranged the bunches in large glass vases.

The room, a sort of hall occupying the centre of the house, with beams of timber showing and a huge chimney covered with gleaming brasses, the room was bright and cheerful and open at both fronts: to the east, on the terrace, by a long bay; to the west, by two windows, on the garden, which it overlooked from the height of a first floor.

The walls were covered with War Office maps, Home Office maps, district maps. There was an oak gun-rack with twelve rifles, all alike and of the latest pattern. Beside it, nailed flat to the wall and roughly stitched together, were three dirty, worn, tattered strips of bunting, blue, white and red.

"They look very well: what do you say?" he asked, when he had finished arranging the flowers, as though his wife had been in the room. "And now, I think, a good pipe . . ."

He took out his tobacco-pouch and matches and, crossing the terrace, went and leant against the stone balustrade that edged it.

Hills and valleys mingled in harmonious curves, all green, in places, with the glad green of the meadows, all dark, in others, with the melancholy green of the firs and larches.

At thirty or forty feet below him ran the road that leads from Saint-Élophe up to the Old Mill. It skirted the walls and then dipped down again to the Étang-des-Moines, or Monks' Pool, of which it followed the left bank. Breaking off suddenly, it narrowed into a rugged path which could be seen in the distance, standing like a ladder against a rampart, and which plunged into a narrow pass between two mountains wilder in appearance and rougher in outline than the ordinary Vosges landscape. This was the Col du Diable, or Devil's Pass, situated

at a distance of sixteen hundred yards from the Old
Mill, on the same level.

A few buildings clung to one of the sides of the
pass: these belonged to Saboureux's Farm. From
Saboureux's Farm to the Butte-aux-Loups, or
Wolves' Knoll, which you saw on the left, you could
make out or imagine the frontier by following a
line of which Morestal knew every guiding-mark,
every turn, every acclivity and every descent.

" The frontier!" he muttered. " The frontier
here . . . at twenty-five miles from the Rhine . . .
the frontier in the very heart of France!"

Every day and ten times a day, he tortured himself in this manner, gazing at that painful and re-
lentless line; and, beyond it, through vistas which
his imagination contrived as it were to carve out of
the Vosges, he conjured up a vision of the German
plain on the misty horizon.

And this too he repeated to himself; and he did
so this time as at every other time, with a bitterness
which the years that passed did nothing to allay:

" The German plain . . . the German hills . . .
all that land of Alsace in which I used to wander as
a boy. . . . The French Rhine, which was my river
and the river of my fathers. . . . And now
Deutschland . . . Deutsches Rhein. . . ."

A faint whistle made him start. He leant over
towards the staircase that climbed the terrace, a

staircase cut out of the rock, by which people coming from the side of the frontier often entered his grounds so as to avoid the bend of the road.   There was nobody there nor anybody opposite, on the roadside slope all tangled with shrubs and ferns.

And the sound was renewed, discreetly, stealthily, with the same modulations as before.

" It's he . . . it's he . . ." thought M. Morestal, with an uncomfortable feeling of embarrassment.

A head popped from between the bushes, a head in which all the bones stood out, joined by prominent muscles, which gave it the look of the head of an anatomical model.   On the bridge of the nose, a pair of copper-rimmed spectacles.   Across the face, like a gash, the toothless, grinning mouth.

" You again, Dourlowski. . . ."

" Can I come? " asked the man.

" No . . . no . . . you're mad. . . ."

" It's urgent."

" Impossible. . . . And besides, you know, I don't want any more of it.   I've told you so before. . . ."

But the man insisted:

" It's for this evening, for to-night. . . . It's a soldier of the Börsweilen garrison. . . . He says he's sick of wearing the German uniform."

" A deserter. . . . I've had enough of them. . . . Shut up and clear out! "

" Now don't be nasty, M. Morestal. . . . Just
think it over. . . . Look here, let's meet at four
o'clock, in the pass, near Saboureux's Farm . . .
like last time. . . . I shall expect you. . . . We'll
have a talk . . . and I shall be surprised if . . ."

" Hold your tongue! " said Morestal.

A voice cried from the drawing-room:

" Here they come, sir, here they come! "

It was the man-servant; and Mme. Morestal also
ran out and said:

" What are you doing here? Whom were you
talking to? "

" Nobody."

" Why, I heard you! . . ."

" No, I assure you. . . ."

" Well, I must have imagined it. . . . I say you
were quite right. It's twelve o'clock and they are
here, the two of them."

" Philippe and Marthe? "

" Yes, they are coming. They are close to the
garden-entrance. Let's hurry down and meet
them. . . ."

CHAPTER II

" He hasn't changed a bit. . . . His complexion is as fresh as ever. . . . The eyes are a little tired, perhaps . . . but he's looking very well. . . ."

" When you've finished picking me to pieces, between you! " said Philippe, laughing. " What an inspection! Why don't you give my wife a kiss? That's more to the point! "

Marthe flung herself into Mme. Morestal's arms and into her father-in-law's and was examined from head to foot in her turn.

" I say, I say, we're thinner in the face than we were! . . . We want picking up. . . . But, my poor children, you're soaked to the skin! "

" We were out all through the storm," said Philippe.

" And what do you think happened to me? " asked Marthe. " I got frightened! . . . Yes, frightened, like a little girl . . . and I fainted. . . . And Philippe had to carry me . . . for half an hour at least. . . ."

" What do you say to that? " said Morestal to

his wife. "For half an hour! He's the same strong chap he was. . . . And why didn't you bring the boys? It's a pity. Two fine little fellows, I feel sure. And well brought up too: I know my Marthe! . . . How old are they now? Ten and nine, aren't they? By the way, mother got two rooms ready. Do you have separate rooms now?"

"Oh, no," said Marthe, "only down here! . . . Philippe wants to get up before day-break and ramble about the roads . . . whereas I need a little rest."

"Capital! Capital! Show them to their rooms, mother . . . and, when you're ready, children, come down to lunch. As soon as we've finished, I'll take the carriage and go and fetch your trunks at Saint-Élophe: the railway-omnibus will have brought them there by this time. And, if I meet my friend Jorancé, I'll bring him back with me. I expect he's in the dumps. His daughter left for Lunéville this morning. But she said she had written to you. . . ."

"Yes," said Marthe, "I had a letter from Suzanne the other day. She didn't seem to like the idea, either, of going away. . . ."

* * *

Two hours later, Philippe and his wife settled themselves in two pretty, adjoining bedrooms on the second floor, looking out on the French side. Marthe threw herself on her bed and fell asleep almost immediately, while her husband, with his elbows on the window-sill, sat gazing at the peaceful valley where the happiest days of his boyhood had been spent.

It was over yonder, in the straggling village of Saint-Élophe-la-Côte, in the modest dwelling which his parents occupied before they moved to the Old Mill. He was at the boarding-school at Noirmont and used to have glorious holidays playing in the village or roaming about the Vosges with his father: Papa Trompette, as he always called him, because of all the trumpets, bugles, horns and cornets which, together with drums of every shape and kind, swords and dirks, helmets and breast-plates, guns and pistols, were the only presents that his childhood knew. Morestal was a little strict; a little too fond of everything that had to do with principle, custom, discipline, exactness; a little quick-tempered; but, at the same time, he was the kindest of men and had no difficulty in winning his son's love, his frank and affectionate respect.

Their only quarrel was on the day when Philippe, who was then in the top form, announced his intention of continuing his studies after he had passed his examination and of entering the Normal School. The father's whole dream was shattered, his great

dream of seeing Philippe in uniform, with his sword
at his side and the gold braid on the sleeve of his
loose jacket.

It came as a violent and painful shock; and
Morestal was stupefied to find himself faced by an
obstinate, deliberate Philippe, a Philippe wholly
master of himself and firmly resolved to lead his
life according to his own views and his own ambi-
tions. For a week on end, the two argued, hurt
each other's feelings, made it up again, only to fall
out once more. Then the father suddenly yielded,
in the middle of a discussion and as though he had
all at once realized the futility of his efforts:

"You have made up your mind?" he cried.
"Very well! An usher you shall be, since that is
your ideal; but I warn you that I decline all responsibility for the future and that I wash my hands of
anything that happens."

What happened was simply that Philippe's career
was swift and brilliant and that, after a probation-
ary term at Lunéville and another at Châteauroux,
he was appointed professor of history at Versailles.
He then published, at a few months' interval, two
remarkable books, which caused much heated con-
troversy: *The Idea of Country in Ancient Greece*
and *The Idea of Country before the Revolution.*
Three years later, he was promoted to Paris, to the
Lycée Carnot.

Philippe was now approaching his fortieth year. Day-work and night-work seemed to have no effect upon his sturdy highland constitution. Possessing a set of powerful muscles and built on the same strong lines as his father, he found rest and recreation from study in violent exercise, in long bicycle-rides into the country or through the woods on the outskirts of Paris. The boys at the school, who held him in a sort of veneration, told stories of his exploits and his feats of strength.

With all this, a great look of gentleness, especially about the eyes, a pair of very good, blue eyes, which smiled when he spoke and which, when at rest, were candid, childish almost, filled with dreams and kindness.

By this time, old Morestal was proud of his son. On the day when he heard of his nomination to Carnot, he wrote, frankly:

"Well done, my dear Philippe! So you're prospering now and in a fair way to obtain anything you like to ask for. Let me tell you that I am not in the least surprised, for I always expected that, with your great qualities, your perseverance and your serious way of looking at life, you would win the place which you deserved. So, once more, well done!

"I confess, however, that your last book, on the

idea of country in France, puzzled me not a little.
I know, of course, that you will not change your
opinions on this subject; but it seems to me that you
are trying to explain the idea of patriotism as due
to rather inferior motives and that this idea strikes
you not as natural and inherent to human societies,
but as though it were a momentary and passing
phase of civilization.   No doubt I have misunder-
stood you.   Still, your book is not very clear.   You
almost appear to be hesitating.   I shall look forward eagerly to the new work, on the idea of country in our own times and in the future, which I see
that you are announcing. . . ."

The book to which Morestal alluded had been
finished for over a year, during which Philippe, for
reasons which he kept to himself, refused to deliver
the manuscript to his publishers.

" Are you glad to be here? "

Marthe had come up and folded her two hands
over his arm.

" Very," he said.   " And I should be still more
pleased if I had not that explanation with my father
before me . . . the explanation which I came down
here to have."

" It will be all right, my own Philippe. Your father is so fond of you. And then you are so sincere! . . ."

" My dear Marthe," he said, kissing her affectionately on the forehead.

He had first met her at Lunéville, through M. Jorancé, who was her distant cousin; and he had at once felt that she was the ideal companion of his life, who would stand by him in hours of trouble, who would bear him comely children, who would understand how to bring them up and how, with his assistance and with his principles, to make sturdy men of them, worthy to bear his name.

Perhaps Marthe would have liked something more; perhaps, as a girl, she had dreamt that a married woman is not merely the wife and mother, but also her husband's lover. But she soon saw that love went for little with Philippe, a studious man, much more interested in mental speculation and social problems than in any manifestation of sentimental feeling. She therefore loved him as he wished to be loved, stifling within herself, like smothered flames, a whole throbbing passion made up of unsatisfied longings, restrained ardours and needless jealousies and allowing only just so much of this to escape her as was needed to give him fresh courage at times of doubt and defeat.

Short, slender and of delicate build, she was

plucky, hardened to trouble, fearless in the face of
obstacles, proof against disappointment after a
check.   Her bright, dark eyes betokened her energy.
In spite of all the influence which Philippe wielded
over her, in spite of the admiration with which he
inspired her, she retained her personality, her own
standpoint towards life, her likes and dislikes.   And,
to such a man as Philippe, nothing could be more
precious.

" Won't you try and sleep a little? " she asked.

" No.   I am going down to him."

" To your father? " she asked, anxiously.

" Yes, I don't want to put it off any longer.   As
it is, I have almost done wrong in coming here and
embracing him without first letting him know the
exact truth about me."

They were silent for a while.   Philippe seemed
undecided and worried.

He said to her:

" Don't you agree with me?   Or do you think
I ought to wait till to-morrow? . . ."

She opened the door for him to pass:

" No," she said, " you are right."

She often had those unexpected movements which
cut short hesitation and put you face to face with
events.   Another would have launched out into
words.   But Marthe never shirked responsibility,
even where it concerned but the smallest facts of

ordinary life.   Philippe used to laugh and call it her daily heroism.

He kissed her and felt strengthened by her confidence.

Downstairs, he was told that his father was not yet back and he resolved to wait for him in the drawing-room.   He lit a cigarette, let it go out again and, at first in a spirit of distraction and then with a growing interest, looked around him, as though he were trying to gather from inanimate objects particulars relating to the man who lived in their midst.

He examined the rack containing the twelve rifles. They were all loaded, ready for service.   Against what foe?

He saw the flag which he had so often gazed upon in the old house at Saint-Élophe, the old, torn flag whose glorious history he knew so well.

He saw the maps hanging on the wall, all of which traced the frontier in its smallest details, together with the country adjoining it on either side of the Vosges.

He bent over the shelves of the little book-case and read the titles of the works: *The War of 1870, prepared in the historical section of the German General Staff; The Retreat of Bourbaki; The Way to prepare our Revenge; The Crime of the Peace-at-any-Price Party. . . .*

But one volume caught his attention more particularly. It was his own book on the idea of country. He turned the pages and, seeing that some of them were covered and scored with pencil-marks, he sat down and began to read:

"It's as I thought," he muttered, presently. "How are he and I to understand each other henceforth? What common ground is there between us? I cannot expect him to accept my ideas. And how can I submit to his?"

He went on reading and noticed comments the harshness of which distressed him beyond measure. Twenty minutes passed in this way, disturbed by no sound but that of the leaves which he turned as he read.

And, suddenly, he felt two bare arms round his head, two cool, bare arms stroking his face. He tried to release himself. The two arms clasped him all the tighter.

He made an abrupt effort and rose to his feet:

"You!" he cried, stepping back. "You here, Suzanne!"

A most attractive creature stood before him, at once smiling and bashful, in an attitude of provocation and fear, with hands clasped, then with arms again outstretched, beautiful, white, fragrant arms that showed below the short sleeves of her fine cambric blouse. Her fair hair was divided into two loose waves, whose rebellious curls played about at random. She had grey, almond-shaped eyes, half-veiled by their dark lashes; and her tiny teeth laughed at the edge of her red lips, lips so red that one would have thought — and been quite wrong in thinking — that they were painted.

It·was Suzanne Jorancé, the daughter of Jorancé the special commissary and a friend of Marthe, who knew her when she was quite a child at Lunéville. Suzanne had spent four months, last winter, in Paris with the Philippe Morestals.

"You!" he repeated. "You, Suzanne!"

She replied, gaily:

"Myself. Your father came to call on us at Saint-Élophe. And, as mine was out for a walk, he brought me back with him. I have just got out of the carriage. And here I am."

He seized her by the wrists, in a fit of anger, and, in a hollow voice:

"You had no business to be at Saint-Élophe. You wrote to Marthe that you were going away this morning. You ought not to have stayed. You know quite well that you ought not to have stayed."

"Why?" she asked, quite confused.

"Why? Because, at the end of your visit to Paris, you spoke to me in words which I was entitled to interpret . . . which I took to mean . . .

And I would not have come, if you had not written that you were . . ."

He broke off, embarrassed by the violence of his own outburst. The tears stood in Suzanne's eyes and her face had flushed so deep a red that her crimson lips seemed hardly red at all.

Petrified by the words which he had uttered and still more by those which he had been on the verge of uttering, Philippe suddenly, in the girl's presence, felt a need to be gentle and friendly and to make amends for his inexplicable rudeness. An unexpected sense of pity softened him. He took the small, ice-cold hands between his own and said, kindly, with the intonation of a big brother scolding a younger sister:

" Why did you stay, Suzanne? "

" May I tell you, Philippe? "

" Certainly, or I shouldn't ask you," he replied, a little nervously.

" I wanted to see you, Philippe. . . . When I knew that you were coming . . . and that, by delaying my departure by one day . . . just one day . . . You understand, don't you? . . ."

He was silent, rightly thinking that, if he answered the least word, she would at once say something that he did not want to hear. And they no longer knew how to stand opposite each other and they no longer dared look each other in the face.

But Philippe felt those small hands turn warm at the touch of his and felt all the life rush once more through that turbulent young being, like a source that is released and brings back joy and strength and hope.

Steps were heard and a sound of voices rose in the hall outside.

"M. Morestal," Suzanne whispered.

And old Morestal shouted, long before entering the room:

"Where are you, Suzanne? Here's your father coming. Quick, Jorancé, the children are here. Yes, yes, your daughter, too. . . . I brought her back with me from Saint-Élophe. . . . But how did you come? Through the woods?"

Suzanne slipped on a pair of long suède gloves and, at the moment when the door opened, said, in a tone of implacable resolve and as though the promise must needs fill Philippe's heart with delight:

"No one shall ever see my bare arms again. . . . No one, Philippe, I swear to you. . . . No one shall ever stroke them. . . ."

CHAPTER III

THE VIOLET PAMPHLET

JORANCÉ was a heavy and rather unwieldy, pleasant-faced man. Twenty-five years before, when secretary to the commissary at Noirmont, he had married a girl of entrancing beauty, who used to teach the piano in a boarding-school. One evening, after four years of marriage, four years of torture, during which the unhappy man suffered every sort of humiliation, Jorancé came home to find the house empty. His wife had gone without a word of explanation, taking their little girl, Suzanne, with her.

The only thing that kept him from suicide was the hope of recovering the child and saving her from the life which her mother's example would have forced upon her in the future.

He did not have to look for her long. A month later, his wife sent back the child, who was no doubt in her way. But the wound had cut deep and lingered; and neither time nor the love which he bore his daughter could wipe out the memory of that cruel story.

He buckled to his work, accepted the most burdensome tasks so as to increase his income and give Suzanne a good education, was transferred to the commissary's office at Lunéville and, somewhat late in life, was promoted to be special commissary at the frontier. The position involved the delicate functions of a sentry on outpost duty whose business it is to see as much as possible of what goes on in the neighbour's country; and Jorancé filled it so conscientiously, tactfully and skilfully that the neighbour aforesaid, while dreading his shrewdness and insight, respected his character and his professional qualities.

At Saint-Élophe, he renewed his intimacy with old Morestal, who was his grand-uncle by marriage and who was very much attached to him.

The two men saw each other almost every day. Jorancé and Suzanne used to dine at the Old Mill on Thursdays and Sundays. Suzanne would also often come alone and accompany the old man on his daily walk. He took a great fancy to her; and it was upon his advice and at the urgent request of Philippe and Marthe Morestal that Jorancé had taken Suzanne to Paris the previous winter.

His first words on entering the room were to thank Philippe:

"You can't think, my dear Philippe, how glad I was to leave her with you. Suzanne is young. And I approve of a little distraction."

He looked at Suzanne with the fervent glance of a father who has brought up his daughter himself and whose love for her is mingled with a touch of feminine affection.

And he said to Philippe:

"Have you heard the news? I am marrying her."

"Really?" said Philippe.

"Yes, to one of my cousins at Nancy, a man rather well-on in years, perhaps, but a serious, active and intelligent fellow. Suzanne likes him very much. You do like him very much, don't you, Suzanne?"

The girl seemed not to hear the question and asked:

"Is Marthe in her room, Philippe?"

"Yes, on the second floor."

"I know, the blue room. I was here yesterday, helping Mme. Morestal. I must run up and give her a kiss."

She turned round in the doorway and kissed her hand to the three men, keeping her eyes fixed on Philippe.

"How pretty and charming your daughter is!" said Morestal to Jorancé.

But they could see that he was thinking of something else and that he was eager to change the conversation. He shut the door quickly and, returning to the special commissary, said:

" Did you come by the frontier-road? "

" No."

" And you haven't been told yet? "

" What? "

" The German post . . . at the Butte-aux-Loups. . . ."

" Knocked down? "

" Yes."

" Oh, by Jove! "

Morestal stopped to enjoy the effect which he had produced and then continued:

" What do you say to it? "

" I say . . . I say that it's most annoying. . . . They're in a very bad temper as it is, on the other side. This means trouble for me."

" Why? "

" Well, of course. Haven't you heard that they're beginning to accuse me of encouraging the German deserters? "

" Nonsense! "

" I tell you, they are. It seems that there's a secret desertion-office in these parts. I'm supposed to be at the head of it. And you, you are the heart and soul of it."

" Oh, they can't stand me at any price ! "

" Nor me either. Weisslicht, the German commissary at Börsweilen, has sworn a mortal hatred against me. We cut each other now when we meet. There's not a doubt but that he is responsible for the calumnies."

" But what proofs do they put forward ? "

" Any number . . . all equally bad. . . . Among others, this : pieces of French gold which are said to have been found on their soldiers. So you see . . . with the post tumbling down once more, the explanations that are certain to begin all over again, the enquiries that are certain to be opened. . . ."

Philippe went up to him :

" Come, come, I don't suppose it's so serious as all that."

" You think not, my boy ? Then you haven't seen the stop-press telegrams in this morning's papers ? "

" No," said Philippe and his father. " What's the news ? "

" An incident in Asia Minor. A quarrel between the French and German officials. One of the consuls has been killed."

" Oh, oh ! " said Morestal. " This time . . ."

And Jorancé went into details :

" Yes, the position is exceedingly strained. The Morocco question has been opened again. Then

there's the espionage business and the story of the
French air-men flying over the fortresses in Alsace
and dropping tricolour flags in the Strasburg streets.
. . . For six months, it has been one long series of
complications and shocks. The newspapers are becoming aggressive in their language. Both countries are arming, strengthening their defences. In
short, in spite of the good intentions of the two
governments, we are at the mercy of an accident.
A spark . . . and the thing's done."

A heavy silence weighed upon the three men.
Each of them conjured up the sinister vision according to his own temperament and instincts.

Jorancé repeated:

" A spark . . . and the thing's done."

" Well, let it be done! " said Morestal, with an
angry gesture.

Philippe gave a start:

" What are you saying, father? "

" Well, what! There must be an end to all this."

" But the end need not be in blood."

" Nonsense . . . nonsense. . . . There are injur-
ies that can only be wiped out in blood. And, when
a great country like ours has received a slap in the
face like that of 1870, it can wait forty years, fifty
years, but a day comes when it returns the slap in
the face . . . and with both hands! "

" And suppose we are beaten? " said Philippe.

"Can't be helped! Honour comes first! Besides, we sha'n't be beaten. Let every man do his duty and we shall see! In 1870, as a prisoner of war, I gave my word not to serve in the French army again. I escaped, I collected the young rapscallions of Saint-Élophe and round about, the old men, the cripples, the women even. . . . We took to the woods. Three rags served as a rallying-signal: a bit of white linen, a strip of red flannel and a piece out of a blue apron . . . the flag of the band! There it hangs. . . . It shall see the light of day again, if necessary."

Jorancé could not help laughing:

"Do you think that will stop the Prussians?"

"Don't laugh, my friend. . . . You know the view I take of my duty and what I am doing. But it is just as well that Philippe should know, too. Sit down, my boy."

He himself sat down, put aside the pipe which he was smoking and began, with the obvious satisfaction of a man who is at last able to speak of what he has most at heart:

"You know the frontier, Philippe, or rather the German side of the frontier? . . . A craggy cliff, a series of peaks and ravines which make this part of the Vosges an insuperable rampart. . . ."

"Yes, absolutely insuperable," said Philippe.

"That's a mistake!" exclaimed Morestal. "A

fatal mistake! From the first moment when I
began to think of these matters, I believed that a
day would come when the enemy would attack that
rampart."

" Impossible ! "

" That day has come, Philippe. For the last six
months, not a week has passed without my meeting
some suspicious figure over there or knocking up
against men walking about in smocks that were
hardly enough to conceal their uniform. . . . It is
a constant, progressive underhand work. Everybody is helping in it. The electric factory which
the Wildermann firm has run up in that ridiculous
fashion on the edge of the precipice is only a make-
believe. The road that leads to it is a military road.
From the factory to the Col du Diable is less than
half a mile. One effort and the frontier's crossed."

" By a company," objected Jorancé.

" Where a company passes, a regiment can pass
and a brigade can follow. . . . At Börsweilen, five
miles from the Vosges, there are three thousand
German soldiers: on a war-footing, mark you. At
Gernach, twelve miles further, there are twelve
thousand; and four thousand horses; and eight hundred waggons. By the evening of the day on which
war is declared, perhaps even earlier, those fifteen
thousand men will have crossed the Col du Diable.
It's not a surprise which they mean to attempt: that

wouldn't be worth their while. It is the absolute
crossing of the frontier, the taking possession of
our ridges, the occupation of Saint-Élophe. When
our troops arrive, it will be too late! They will
find Noirmont cut off, Belfort threatened, the south
of the Vosges invaded. . . . You can picture the
moral effect: we shall be done for! That is what
is being prepared in the dark. That is what you
have been unable to see, Jorancé, in spite of all your
watchfulness . . . and in spite of my warnings."

" I wrote to the prefect last week."

" You should have written last year! All this
time, the other has been coming on, the other has
been advancing. . . . He hardly takes the trouble
to conceal himself. . . . There . . . listen to him
. . . listen to him. . . ."

In the far distance, like the sound of an echo,
deadened by the mass of trees, a bugle-call had rung
out, somewhere, through the air. It was an indis-
tinct call, but Morestal was not mistaken and he
hissed:

" Ah, it's he! . . . It's he. . . . I know the voice
of Germany. . . . I know it when I hear it . . .
the hoarse, the odious voice! . . ."

Presently, Philippe, who had not taken his eyes
off his father, said:

" And then, father?"

" And then, my son, it was in anticipation of that

day that I built my house on this hill, that I surrounded my gardens with a wall, that, unknown to
anybody, I stocked the out-houses with means of
defence: ammunition, bags of sand, gun-powder
. . . that, in short, I prepared for an alarm by setting up this unsuspected little fortress at twenty minutes from the Col du Diable . . . on the very
threshold of the frontier!"

He had planted himself with his face to the east,
with his face to the enemy; and, clutching his hips
with his clenched hands, in an attitude of defiance,
he seemed to be awaiting the inevitable assault.

The special commissary, who still feared that his
zeal had been caught napping in this business,
growled:

"Your shanty won't hold out for an hour."

"And who tells you," shouted Morestal, "who
tells you that that hour is not exactly the one hour
which we shall want to gain? . . . An hour! You
never spoke a truer word: an hour of resistance to
the first attack! An hour of delay! . . . That's
what I wanted, that's what I offer to my country.
Let every one be doing as I am, to the best of his
power, let every one be haunted to fever-point by
the obsession of the personal service which it is his
duty to render to the country; and, if war breaks
out, you shall see how a great nation can take its
revenge!"

" And suppose we are beaten, in spite of all?"
Philippe asked again.

" What's that?"

Old Morestal turned to his son as though he had
received a blow; and a rush of blood inflamed his
features.   He looked Philippe in the face:

" What do you say?"

Philippe had an inkling of the conflict that would
hurl them one against the other if he dared to state
his objections more minutely.   And he uttered
words at random:

" Of course, the supposition is not one of those
which we can entertain. . . . But, all the same . . .
don't you think we ought to face the possibility? . . ."

" Face the possibility of defeat?" echoed the old
man, who seemed thunderstruck.   " Are you sug-
gesting that the fear of that ought to influence
France in her conduct?"

A diversion relieved Philippe of his difficulty.
Some one had appeared from the staircase at the
end of the terrace and in so noisy a fashion that
Morestal did not wait for his son to reply:

" Is that you, Saboureux?   What a row you're
making!"

It was Farmer Saboureux, whose house could be
seen on the Col du Diable.   He was accompanied by
an old, ragged tramp.

Saboureux had come to complain. Some
soldiers taking part in the manœuvres had helped
themselves to two of his chickens and a duck.
He seemed beside himself, furious at the catastrophe:

"Only, I've a witness in old Poussière here.
And I want an indemnity, not to speak of damages
and punishment. I call it a calamity, I do: soldiers
of our own country! . . . I'm a good Frenchman,
but, all the same . . ."

Morestal was too much absorbed in the discussion
of his favourite ideas to take the least interest in the
man's troubles; and the farmer's presence, on the
contrary, seemed to him an excellent reason for returning to the subject in hand. They had other
things to talk about than chickens and ducks! What
about the chances of war? And the alarming ru-
mours that were current?

"What do you say, Saboureux?"

The farmer presented the typical appearance of
those peasants whom we sometimes find in the
eastern provinces and who, with their stern, clean-
shaven faces, like the faces on ancient medals, remind us of our Roman ancestors rather than of the
Gauls or Francs. He had marched to battle in 1870
with the others, perishing with hunger and wretchedness, risking his skin. And, on his return, he had
found his shanty reduced to ashes. Some passing

Uhlans. . . . Since that time, he had laboured hard to repair the harm done.

"And you want it all over again?" he said. "More Uhlans burning and sacking? . . . Oh, no, I've had enough of that game! You just let me be as I am!"

He was filled with the small land-owner's hatred against all those, Frenchmen or others, who were likely to tread with a sacrilegious foot on the sown earth, where the harvest is so slow in coming. He crossed his arms, with a serious air.

"And you, Poussière, what would you say if we went to war?" asked Morestal, calling to the old tramp, who was sitting on the parapet of the terrace, breaking a crust.

The man was lean and wizened, twisted like a vine-shoot, with long, dust-coloured hair and a melancholy, impassive face that seemed carved out of old oak. He put in an appearance at Saint-Élophe once every three or four months. He knocked at the doors of the houses and then went off again.

"What country do you belong to, to begin with?"

He grunted:

"Don't know much about it . . . it's so long ago. . . ."

"Which do you like best? France, eh? The roads on this side?"

The old chap swung his legs without answering, perhaps without understanding. Saboureux grinned:

"He doesn't look at the roads, not he! He doesn't as much as know if he belongs to the country on the right or on the left! His country lies where the grub lies . . . eh, Poussière?"

Thereupon, seized with sudden ill-humour, Morestal lost his temper and let fly at the lukewarm, at the indifferent — working-men, townsmen or farmers — who think only of their comfort, without caring whether the country is humiliated or victorious. But what else could one expect, with the detestable ideas spread by some of the newspapers and carried to the furthermost ends of the country in the books and pamphlets hawked about by travelling agents?

"Yes," he cried, "the new ideas: those are the evil that is destroying us. The school-masters are poisoning the minds of the young. The very army is smitten with the canker. Whole regiments are on the verge of mutiny. . . ."

He turned a questioning glance upon Philippe, who, from time to time, nodded his head without replying, with a movement which his father might take for one of approval.

"Isn't it so, Philippe? You see the thing close at hand, where you are: all those poltroons who weaken our energies with their fine dreams of peace at any price! You hear them, all the wind-bags at the public meetings, who preach their loathsome crusade against the army and the country with open doors and are backed up by our rulers. . . . And that's only speaking of the capital! . . . Why, the very provinces haven't escaped the contagion! . . . Here, have you read this abomination?"

He took a little volume in a violet wrapper from among the papers heaped up on his table and held it before his son's eyes. And he continued:

"*Peace before All!* No author's name. A book that's all the more dangerous because it's very well written, not by one of those wind-bags to whom I was referring just now, but by a scholar, a provincial and, what's more, a Frenchman from the frontier. He seems even to bear our name . . . some distant cousin, no doubt: the Morestals are a large family."

"Are you sure?" blurted Philippe, who had turned pale at the sight of the pamphlet. "How do you know?"

"Oh, by accident. . . . A letter which was addressed to me and which said, 'All good wishes for the success of your pamphlet, my dear Morestal.'"

Philippe remembered. He was to have gone to the Old Mill last year; and the letter must have been sent to him by one of his friends.

"And haven't you tried to find out?"

"What for? Because I have a scoundrel in my family, that's no reason why I should be in a hurry to make his acquaintance! Besides, he himself has had the decency not to put his name to his scurrilous nonsense. . . . No matter: if ever I lay my hands on him! . . . But don't let's talk of it. . . ."

He continued to talk of it, nevertheless, and at great length, as well as of all the questions of war and peace, history and politics that came to his mind. It was not until he had "got his budget off his chest," as he said, that he exclaimed, suddenly:

"Enough of this palavering, my friends! Why, it's four o'clock! Saboureux, I'm your man. . . . So they've been making free with your poultry, have they? Are you coming, Jorancé? We'll see some fine soldier-chaps making their soup. There's nothing jollier and livelier than a French camp!"

CHAPTER IV

PHILIPPE AND HIS WIFE

MARTHE and Suzanne were very intimate, in spite
of the difference in their ages. Marthe was full
of indulgent kindness for her friend, whom she had
known as quite a child, motherless and left to herself; whereas Suzanne was less even-tempered with
Marthe, now gushing and coaxing, now aggressive
and satirical, but always full of charm.

When Marthe had finished unfastening the
trunks, Suzanne herself insisted on emptying the
travelling-bag and arranging on the table all the little things with which one tries, when away, to
give one's room a look of home: portraits of the
children, writing-cases, favourite books. . . .

" You'll be very snug here, Marthe," she said.
" It's a nice, light room . . . and there's only a
dressing-room between you and Philippe. . . . But
how did you come to want two bedrooms? "

" It was Philippe. He was afraid of disturbing
me in the mornings. . . ."

" Oh," repeated the girl. " It was Philippe's suggestion. . . ."

Then she took up one of the photographs and examined it:

" How like his father your son Jacques is! . . . Much more so than Paul . . . don't you think? "

Marthe came to the table and, bending over her friend, looked at the picture with those mother's eyes which seem to see in the inanimate image the life, the smile and the beauty of the absent one.

" Which do you like best, Jacques or Paul? " asked Suzanne.

" What a question! If you were a mother. . . ."

" If I were a mother, I should like that one best who reminded me most of my husband. The other would make me suspect that my husband had ceased to love me. . . ."

" You put down everything to love, my poor Suzanne! Do you imagine that there is nothing in the world but love? "

" There are heaps of other things. But you yourself, Marthe: wouldn't you like love to fill a greater place in your life? "

This was said with a certain sarcasm, of which Marthe felt the sting. But, before she had time to retort, Philippe appeared in the doorway.

Suzanne at once cried:

" We were talking about you, Philippe."

He made no reply. He went to the window, closed it and then came back to the two young

women. Suzanne pointed to a chair beside her, but
he sat down by Marthe; and Marthe saw by his look
that something had happened:

" Have you spoken to him? "

" No."

" Still . . ."

He told her, in a few sentences, of the conversation, with the incident of the pamphlet and the
words which his father had spoken against the author of that work. He repeated the words, a second time, with increasing bitterness. Then he
stopped, reflected and, pressing his clenched fists to
his temples, said, slowly, as though he were explain-
ing matters to himself:

" It's three years now that this has lasted . . .
ever since his letter on my appointment, in which
he wrote about my second book on the idea of
country. Perhaps I ought to have written to him
then and there and told him of the evolution of my
mind and the tremendous change which the study
of history and of vanished civilizations had wrought
in me."

" Perhaps it would have been better," said
Marthe.

" I was afraid to. I was afraid of hurting him.
. . . It would have hurt him so terribly! . . . And
my love for him is so great! . . . And then,
Marthe, you see, the ideas which he defends and

of which, in my eyes, he is the living and splendid
incarnation are so beautiful in themselves that, after
one has ceased to share them, one continues, for a
long time, for always, to retain a sort of involuntary affection for them, deep down in one's inner
self. They constituted the greatness of our country
for centuries. They are vigorous, like everything
that is religious and pure. One feels a renegade at
losing them; and any word spoken against them
sounds like blasphemy. How could I say to my
father, ' Those ideas, which you gave me and which
were the life of my youth, I have ceased to hold.
Yes, I have ceased to think as you do. My love of
humanity does not stop at the boundaries of the
country in which I was born; and I do not hate
those who are on the other side of the frontier. I
am one of those men who will not have war, who
will not have it at any price and who would give
their life-blood to save the world the horror of that
scourge.' How could I say such things as that to
my father?"

He rose and, pacing the room, continued:

" I did not say them. I concealed the true state
of my mind, as though I were hiding a shameful
sore. At the meetings, in the newspapers to which
I contribute by stealth, to my adversaries and to the
majority of the men on my own side I was M.
Philippe, denying my name and my personality, set-

ting a bad example to those who are silent for prudence' sake and for fear of compromising themselves.   I do not sign the pamphlets which I write;
and the book in which I give the conclusion of my
work has been ready for more than a year, without
my daring to publish it.   Well, that's over now.   I
can't go on as I have been doing.   Silence is choking me.   By humbling myself, I lower my ideals.
I must speak aloud, in the hearing of all men.   I
will speak."

He had gradually become animated, excited by
his own words.   His voice had increased in volume.   His face expressed the glowing, irresistible,
often blind enthusiasm of those who devote themselves to generous causes.   And, yielding to a need
to speak out which was anything but frequent with
him, he went on:

"You don't know, you don't know what it means
to a man to be fired with a great idea . . . whether
it be love of humanity, hatred of war or any other
beautiful illusion.   It lights us and leads us.   It is
our pride and our faith.   We seem to have a second
life, the real life, that belongs to it, and an unknown heart that beats for it alone.   And we are
prepared to suffer any sacrifice, any pain, any
wretchedness, any insult . . . provided that it gain
the day."

Suzanne listened to him with obvious admiration.

Marthe appeared uneasy. Knowing Philippe's nature thoroughly, she was well aware that, in thus letting himself go, he was not only being carried away by a flood of eloquent words.

He opened the window and drew a deep breath of the pure air which he loved. Then he returned and added:

"We are even prepared to sacrifice those around us."

Marthe felt all the importance which he attached to this little sentence; and, after a moment, she said:

"Are you referring to me?"

"Yes," said Philippe.

"But you know, Philippe, that, when I agreed to marry you, I agreed to share your life, whatever it might be."

"My life as it looked like being, but not as I shall be compelled to make it."

She looked at him with a glimmer of apprehension. For some time now, she had noticed that he was even less communicative than usual, that he hardly ever spoke of his plans and that he no longer told her what he was working at.

"How do you mean, Philippe?" she asked.

He took a sealed letter from his pocket and showed her the address:

"*To the Minister of Public Instruction.*"

" What is in that letter? " asked Marthe.

" My resignation."

" Your resignation! The resignation of your professorship? "

" Yes. I shall send this letter the moment I have confessed everything to my father. I did not like to tell you before, for fear of your objections. . . . But I was wrong. . . . It is necessary that you should know. . . ."

" I don't understand," she stammered. " I don't understand. . . ."

" Yes, you do, Marthe: you understand. The ideas which have taken possession of me little by little and to which I want to devote myself without reserve are dangerous for young brains to listen to. They form the belief of an age for which I call with might and main, but it is not the belief of to-day; and I have no right to teach it to the children entrusted to my care."

She was on the verge — thinking of her own children, whose well-being and whose future were about to suffer through this decision — she was on the verge of exclaiming:

" Why need you shout it from the house-tops? Stifle your vain scruples and go on teaching what you find in the manuals and school-books."

But she knew that he was like those priests who prefer to incur poverty and opprobrium rather than preach a religion which they no longer believe.

And she simply said:

" I do not share all your opinions, Philippe. There are even some that terrify me . . . especially those which I do not know, but which I half suspect. But, whatever the goal to which you are leading us, I will walk to it with my eyes closed."

" And . . . so far . . . you approve? "

" Entirely. You must act according to your conscience, send that letter and, first of all, tell your father everything. Who knows? Perhaps he will admit . . ."

" Never! " exclaimed Philippe. " Men who look into the future can still understand the beliefs of former days, because those were their own beliefs when they were young. But men who cling to the past cannot accept ideas which they do not understand and which clash with their feelings and with their instincts."

" So . . .? "

" So we shall quarrel and cause each other pain; and the thought of it distresses me infinitely."

He sat down, with a movement of weariness. She leant over him:

" Do not lose courage. I am sure that things will turn out better than you think. Wait a few days. . . . There is no hurry; and you will have time to see . . . to prepare. . . ."

" Everything turns out well when you speak," he said, smiling and allowing himself to be caressed.

" Unfortunately . . ."

He did not finish his sentence. He saw Suzanne opposite him, glaring at the pair of them. She was ghastly pale; and her mouth was wrung with a terrible expression of pain and hatred. He felt that she was ready to fling herself upon them and proclaim her rage aloud.

He released himself quickly and, making an effort to jest:

" Tush ! " he said. " Time will show. . . . Enough of these jeremiads : what say you, Suzanne? . . . Suppose you saw to putting away my things? . . . Is everything done? "

Marthe was surprised at the abrupt change in his manner. However, she replied :

" There are only your papers; and I always prefer you to arrange them yourself."

" Come on, then," he said, gaily.

Marthe walked through the dressing-room to her husband's bedroom. Philippe was about to follow her and his foot touched the door-sill when Suzanne darted in front of him and barred the way with her outstretched arms.

It happened so suddenly that he uttered a slight exclamation. Marthe asked, from the further room :

" What is it? "

" Nothing," said Suzanne. " We're coming."

Philippe tried to pass. She pushed him back violently and with such a look of her eyes that he yielded at once.

They watched each other for a few seconds, like two enemies. Philippe fumed:

" Well? What does all this mean? Do you propose to keep me here indefinitely? . . ."

She came nearer to him and, in a voice that shook with restraint and implacable energy:

" I shall expect you this evening. . . . It's quite easy. . . . You can get out. . . . I shall be outside my door at eleven."

He was petrified:

" You are mad! . . ."

" No. . . . But I want to see you . . . to speak to you . . . I must . . . I am suffering more than I can bear . . . It's enough to kill me."

Her eyes were full of tears, her chin seemed convulsed with spasms, her lips trembled.

Philippe's anger was mingled with a little pity; and, above all, he felt the need of putting an end to the scene as quickly as possible:

" Look here, baby, look here! " he said, employing an expression which he often used to her.

" You will come . . . you must come . . . that is why I stayed. . . . One hour, one hour of your presence! . . . If you don't, I shall come here, I shall indeed. . . . I don't care what happens!"

He had retreated to the window. Instinctively, he looked to see if it was possible to climb over the balcony and jump. It would have been absurd.

But, as he bent forward, he saw his wife, two windows further, lean out and catch sight of him. He had to smile, to conceal his perturbation; and nothing could be more hateful to him than this comedy which a child's whims were compelling him to play.

"You're quite pale," said Marthe.

"Do you think so? I'm a little tired, I suppose. You too, you are looking . . ."

She broke in:

"I thought I saw your father."

"Is he back?"

"Yes, there he is, at the end of the garden, with M. Jorancé. They are making signs to you."

Morestal and his friend were climbing up beside the waterfall and waving their hands to attract Philippe's attention. When he came under the windows, Morestal cried:

"This is what we have arranged, Philippe. You and I are dining at Jorancé's."

"But . . ."

"There's no but about it; we'll explain why.

I'll have the carriage got ready and Jorancé will go ahead with Suzanne."

"What about Marthe?" asked Philippe.

"Marthe can come if she likes. Come down here. We'll fix it all up."

When Philippe turned round, Suzanne was standing close against him:

"You'll come, won't you?" she said, eagerly.

"Yes, if Marthe does."

"Even if Marthe doesn't. . . . I insist . . I insist. . . . Oh, Philippe, I implore you, don't drive me to extremities!"

He was afraid of an outburst:

"As a matter of fact," he said, "why shouldn't I come? It's quite natural that I should dine at your house with my father."

"Do you mean it?" she murmured. "Will you really come?"

She seemed suddenly calmed; and her face assumed a look of childish delight:

"Oh, how happy I am! . . . How happy I am! My beautiful dream will be fulfilled. . . . We shall walk together in the dark, without speaking a word. . . . And I shall never forget that hour. . . . Nor you either, Philippe . . . nor you either. . . ."

CHAPTER V

A HAND was passed through the bars of the gate at the top of the staircase leading to the terrace and seized the clapper of the little bell fastened to one of the bars. A push . . . and the gate was open.

" Not much difficulty about that," said the man, carefully stepping on to the terrace. " Since the mountain won't come to Dourlowski, Dourlowski must . . ."

The man stopped: he had heard voices. But, on listening, he found that the sound of voices came from behind the house. He quietly entered the drawing-room, therefore, walked straight across it and reached the windows on the other side. A little further, at the foot of the steps, he saw a carriage ready to start, with Suzanne and her father sitting in it. The Morestal family were standing round the carriage.

" That's all right," said Morestal. " Philippe and I will walk . . . and we'll do the same coming home, won't we, my boy? "

"And you, Marthe?" asked Jorancé.

"No, thank you. I will stay with mamma."

"Well, we'll send your men home to you soon
. . . especially as Morestal likes going to bed early.
They will leave the house at ten o'clock precisely;
and I will go a bit of the way with them, as far as
the Butte."

"That's it," said Morestal. "We shall see the
demolished post by moonlight. And we shall be
here by half-past ten, mother. That's a promise.
Off you go, Victor."

The carriage drove off. Dourlowski, in the
drawing-room, took out his watch and set it by the
clock, whispering:

"Consequently, they'll reach the Butte at a quarter past ten. That's a good thing to know. And
now to inform old Morestal that his friend Dourlowski has come to hunt him up in his happy home."

Putting two of his fingers to his mouth, he gave
the same faint whistle which Morestal had heard
that morning, something like the unfinished note of
certain birds:

"That's done it," he grinned. "The old boy
pricked up his ears. He has sent the others for a
stroll in the garden and he's coming this way. . . ."

He made a movement backwards on hearing
Morestal's footstep in the hall, for he knew the
old fellow was not given to joking. And, in fact,

Morestal, the moment he entered, ran up to him and took him by the collar of his jacket:

" What are you doing here? What do you mean by it? How dare you? . . . I'll show you a road which you don't know of!"

Dourlowski began to laugh with his crooked mouth:

" My dear M. Morestal, you'll dirty your hands."

His clothes were shiny and thick with grease, stretched over a small round body, that contrasted strangely with his lean and bony face. And all this formed a jovial, grotesque and rather alarming picture.

Morestal let go his hold and, in an imperative tone:

" Explain yourself and quickly. I don't want my son to see you here. Speak."

There was no time to be lost, as Dourlowski saw:

" Well, look here," he said. " It's a question of a young soldier in the Börsweilen garrison. He's too unhappy for words where he is . . . and he's mad at having to serve Germany."

" A ne'er-do-well," growled Morestal. " A slacker who doesn't want to work."

" No, not this one, I tell you, not this one. He means to enlist in the Foreign Legion. He loves France."

" Yes, always the same story. And then — pah!

— one never hears of them again.   More gallows'
seed ! "

Dourlowski seemed shocked and scandalized:

" How can you say such a thing, M. Morestal?
. . . If you only knew!   A brave soldier who asks
nothing better than to die fighting for our country."

The old man started:

" ' Our country,' indeed!   I forbid you to speak
like that.   Have you the least idea where you hail
from?   A scamp like you has no country."

" You forget all that I have done, M. Morestal.
. . . You and I, between us, have ' passed ' four of
them already."

" Hold   your   tongue ! "   said   Morestal,   who
seemed to take no pleasure in this recollection.
" Hold your tongue. . . . If the thing had never
happened . . ."

" It would happen just the same, because you
are a good-natured man and because there are
things. . . . There. . . . It's like with this lad.
. . . It would break your heart to see him. . . .
Johann Baufeld his name is. . . . His father is just
dead . . . and he wants to go out to his mother,
who was divorced and who lives in Algeria. . . .
Such a nice lad, full of pluck. . . ."

" Well," said Morestal, " he's only got to ' pass ' !
You don't want me for that."

" And what about the money?   He hasn't a sou.

Besides, there's no one like you to tell us all the paths, the best place to cross at, the best time to select. . . ."

" I'll see about it. . . . I'll see about it," said Morestal. " There's no hurry. . . ."

" Yes, there is. . . ."

" Why? "

" The Börsweilen regiment is manœuvring on the slopes of the Vosges. If you'll lend us a hand, I'll run down to Saint-Élophe first, buy a suit of second-hand French peasant's clothes and go and find my man. Then I'll bring him to the old barn in your little farm to-night . . . as I have done be-fore. . . ."

" Where is he at this moment? "

" His company is quartered in the Albern Woods."

" But that's next door to the frontier!" cried Morestal. " An hour's walk, no more."

" Just so; but how he is to reach the frontier? Where is he to cross it? "

" That's quite easy," said Morestal, taking up a pencil and a sheet of note-paper. " Look, here are the Albern Woods. Here's the Col du Diable. Here's the Butte-aux-Loups. . . . Well, he's only got to leave the woods by the Fontaine-Froide and take the first path to the left, by the Roche de . . ."

He suddenly interrupted himself, looked at Dourlowski with a suspicious air and said:

"But you know the road as well as I do . . .
there's no doubt about that. . . . So . . ."

"My word," said Dourlowski, "I always go by
the Col du Diable and the factory."

Morestal reflected for a moment, scribbled a few
lines and a few words in an absent-minded sort of
way and then, with a movement of quick resolution, took the sheet of note-paper, crumpled it into
a ball and flung it into the waste-paper basket:

"No, no, certainly not!" he cried.   "I've had
enough of this nonsense!   One succeeds four times;
and, at the fifth attempt . . . Besides, it's not a
business I care about. . . . A soldier's a soldier . . .
whatever uniform he wears. . . ."

"Still . . ." mumbled Dourlowski.

"I refuse.   Not to mention that they suspect
me over yonder.   The German commissary gives
me a queer look when he meets me; and I won't
risk . . ."

"You're risking nothing."

"That'll do; and clear out of this as fast as you
can. . . . Oh, wait a second! . . . I think I . . .
Listen . . ."

Morestal ran to the windows overlooking the
garden.   Quick as thought, Dourlowski stooped and
fished Morestal's crumpled sheet out of the waste-

paper basket. He hid it in the palm of his hand and, raising his voice:

"We'll say no more about it, as you don't see your way to help me," he said. "I give it up."

"That's it," said Morestal, who had seen no one in the garden. "You give it up, my friend: it's the best thing you can do."

He took Dourlowski by the shoulders and pushed him towards the terrace:

"Be off . . . and don't come back. . . . There's nothing more for you to do here . . . absolutely nothing. . . ."

He hoped to get rid of the fellow without being perceived, but, as he reached the gate, he saw his wife, his son and Marthe come up the staircase, after strolling round the walls of the Old Mill.

Dourlowski took off his hat and distributed bows all round. Then, as soon as the road was clear, he disappeared.

Mme. Morestal expressed her astonishment:

"What! Do you still see that rogue of a Dourlowski?"

"Oh, it was an accident! . . ."

"You are very wrong to have him in the house. We don't even know where he comes from or what his trade is."

"He's a hawker."

"A spy, rather: that's what they say about him."

" Tah!   In the pay of which country? "

" Of both, very likely.   Victor thinks he saw him with the German commissary, two Sundays ago."

" With   Weisslicht?   Impossible.   He   doesn't even know him."

" I'm telling you what they say.   In any case, Morestal, be careful with that fellow.   He's a bird of ill-omen."

" Come, come, mother, no hard words.   This is a day of rejoicing. . . . Are you ready, Philippe? "

CHAPTER VI

THE PLASTER STATUE

THERE were several ways leading to Saint-Élophe. First of all, the high-road, which goes winding down a slope some two miles long; next, a few rather steep short cuts; and, lastly, further north, the forest-path, part of which skirts the ridge of the Vosges.

" Let's go by the road, shall we? " said Morestal to his son.

And, as soon as they had started, he took Philippe's arm and said, gleefully:

" Only think, my boy, at the camp, just now, we met one of the lieutenants of the manœuvring company. We talked about the Saboureux business and, this evening, he is going to introduce us to his captain, who happens to be a nephew of General Daspry, commanding the army-corps. So I shall tell him what I have done at the Old Mill, you see; he will report it to his uncle Daspry; and Fort Morestal will be listed at once. . . ."

He beamed with delight, held his head high and flung out his chest, while, with his free hand, he made warlike flourishes with his cane. Once he even halted and placed himself on guard and stamped his foot on the ground:

"Three appels . . . Engage . . . Lunge! What do you say to that, Philippe, eh? Old Morestal is game yet!"

Philippe, full of affection for the old man, smiled. Now that he was acting on Marthe's advice and delaying the painful explanation, life seemed better to him, quite simple and quite easy, and he surrendered himself to the pleasure of seeing his father again and the scenes which he loved and renewing the childhood memories that seemed to await him at every turn of the road and to rise up at his approach:

"Do you remember, father? This is where I fell off my bicycle. . . . I was standing under that tree when it was struck by lightning. . . ."

They stopped, recalled all the circumstances of the event and set off again, arm in arm.

And, a little further, Morestal took up the thread:

"And over there, do you remember? That's where you killed your first rabbit . . . with a catapult! Ah, even in those days you promised to be a good shot . . . the best at Saint-Élophe, as I live! . . . But I was forgetting: you have given up your

gun! A fellow of your build! Why, sport, my
boy, is the great apprenticeship for war! . . ."

Saint-Élophe-la-Côte, once a flourishing little
town, had never quite recovered from the wounds
earned by its heroism during the war. It stood
crowding round an old ruined castle which became
visible at the last turn in the road. Nevertheless,
situated on the borders of the department, at twelve
or thirteen miles from Noirmont, the sub-prefecture,
it owed a certain importance to its position near the
frontier, facing the German garrisons, whose increasing activity was becoming a subject of uneasiness and had led to Jorancé's appointment as special
commissary.

Jorancé, the first holder of this newly-created
office, lived at the other end of the village and a
little way outside it, in a low-storeyed house which
had been greatly improved by Suzanne's good taste
and fancy. It was surrounded by a garden with
arbours and quaintly-clipped old trees and a clear,
winding stream that flowed under the very door-
step.

It was nearly dark when Morestal entered, accompanied by Philippe. Everything was ready for
their reception: the table was laid in a room hung
with bright stuffs; flowers were scattered over the

cloth; two lamps shed a calm and even light; and
Suzanne sat smiling, happy and charming.

All this was very simple. And yet Philippe received the impression that special pains had been
taken on his account. It was he who was expected;
he was the master who was to be conquered and
chained with invisible bonds. He felt sure of this;
and Suzanne told him as much throughout dinner,
with her fond glances, her attentive movements, her
whole person bending towards him.

" I ought not to have come," he thought. " No,
I ought not to have."

And, each time that he met Suzanne's eyes, he
called to mind his wife's discreet manner and her
thoughtful air.

" How absorbed you are, Philippe!" cried
Morestal, who had never ceased talking while eating. " And you, Suzanne, what are you thinking
about? Your future husband?"

" Not I!" she replied, without the least embarrassment. " I was thinking of those months I spent
in Paris last winter. How good you were to me,
Philippe! I remember the walks we used to
take! . . ."

They spoke of those walks; and, little by little,
Philippe was surprised to realize the extent to which
their lives had been mingled during that stay.
Marthe, retained by her household duties, used to

remain at home, while they two escaped, like a couple of free and careless play-fellows. They visited the museums and churches of Paris, the little towns and castles of the Ile-de-France. An intimacy sprang up between them. And now it confused him to find Suzanne at once so near to him and so far, so near as a friend, so far as a woman.

When dinner was over, he moved round to his father. Morestal, eager, to go and keep his appointment with Captain Daspry, stood up:

" Are you coming with us, Philippe? "

" Certainly."

The three men took their hats and sticks; but, when they reached the hall-door, after a whispered colloquy with Jorancé, Morestal said to his son:

" On second thoughts, it's better that we should go alone. The interview must remain as secret as possible; and we shall be less easy if there are three of us. . . ."

" Besides," added the special commissary, " you may just as well keep Suzanne company: it is her last evening. Good-bye for the present, children. You can be sure that the two conspirators will be back when the belfry-clock strikes ten, eh, Morestal? "

They went off, leaving Philippe not a little perplexed.

Suzanne burst out laughing:

" My poor Philippe, you look very uncomfortable.   Come, cheer up!   I sha'n't eat you, I promise
you!"

" No, I don't expect you will," he said, laughing
in his turn.   " But, all the same, it's strange . . ."

" All the same, it's strange," she said, completing
the sentence, " that we should take a walk round the
garden together, as I asked you.   You will have to
make the best of a bad job.   Here comes the harm-
less, necessary moonlight."

The moon emerged slowly from the great clouds
stacked around a mountain-crest; and its light cast
the regular shadows of the yews and fir-trees on
the lawns.   The weather was heavy with approaching storms.   A warm breeze wafted the perfumes
of plants and grass.

Three times, they followed the outer path, along
a hedge and along a wall.   They said nothing; and
this silence, which he found it impossible to break,
filled Philippe with remorse.   At that moment, he
experienced a feeling of aversion for that capricious
and unreasonable little girl, who had brought about
those compromising minutes between them.   Unaccustomed to women and always rather shy in their
company, he suspected her of some mysterious de-
sign.

" Let's go over there," said Suzanne, pointing
to the middle of the garden, where the shadows

seemed to gather round a thick clump of shrubs and hornbeams.

They made for the place through an arcade of verdure which brought them to a short flight of steps. It was a sunk amphitheatre, surrounded by a stone balustrade, with a small pond in the middle and, opposite, in a leafy frame, a female statue, with a moonbeam quivering upon it. A musty smell arose from this old-fashioned spot.

"Venus or Minerva? Corinne perhaps?" said Philippe, joking to conceal his uneasiness. "I confess I can't quite make out. What is she wearing: a peplum or an Empire frock? And is that a helmet or a turban on her head?"

"It depends," said Suzanne.

"How do you mean? What upon?"

"Yes, it depends upon my humour. When I'm good and sensible, she's Minerva. When I look at her with a yearning heart, she becomes Venus. And she is also, according to the mood of the moment, the goddess of madness . . . and the goddess of tears . . . and the goddess of death."

She spoke with a playfulness that saddened Philippe. He asked:

"And what is she the goddess of to-day?"

"The goddess of farewell."

"Of farewell?"

"Yes, farewell to Suzanne Jorancé, to the girl

who has come here every day, for the last five years, and who will never come here again."

She leant against the statue:

" My dear goddess, what dreams we two have had, you and I ! We used to wait together. For whom? For the Blue Bird . . . for Prince Charming. The prince was to arrive on horseback, one day, jump the garden-wall and carry me off, slung across his saddle. He was to slip through the trees, one evening, and go up the steps on his knees, sobbing. And all the vows I made to my dear goddess! Just think, Philippe: I promised her never to bring a man into her presence unless I loved him! And I kept my promise. You are the first, Philippe."

He flushed red in the dark; and she continued, in a voice the gaiety of which rang false:

" If you only knew how silly a girl is, dreaming and vowing things! Why, I even promised her that that man and I should exchange our first kiss before her. Isn't it ridiculous? Poor goddess! She will never see that kiss of love; for, after all, I don't suppose you intend to kiss me?"

" Suzanne! "

" Well, did you? There's no reason why you should; and the whole thing's absurd. So you will admit that this dear goddess has no sense and that she deserves to be punished."

With a quick movement of the arm, she gave a push to the statue, which fell to the ground and broke into halves.

"What are you doing?" he cried.

"Leave me alone . . . leave me alone," said Suzanne, in an angry voice.

It was as though her action had loosed in her a long-contained fury and wicked instincts which she was no longer able to control. She rushed forwards and madly kicked and raged at the broken pieces of the statue.

He tried to interfere and took her by the arm. She turned upon him:

"I won't have you touch me! . . . It's your fault. . . . Let me go . . . I hate you! . . . Yes, it's all your fault! . . ."

And, releasing herself from his grasp, she fled towards the house.

The scene had not lasted twenty seconds.

"Hang it!" snarled Philippe, though he was not in the habit of swearing.

His irritation was so great that, if the poor plaster goddess had not already been reduced to fragments, he would certainly have flung her from her pedestal. But, above all things, he was swayed by one idea: to go away, not to see Suzanne again and to have done with this nonsense, of which he felt all the hatefulness and absurdity.

He also quickly made his way back to the house. Unfortunately, knowing no other outlet by which to escape, he went through the passage. The dining-room door was open. He saw the girl sitting huddled in a chair, with her head between her hands, sobbing.

He did not know how artificial a woman's tears can be. Nor did he know the danger in those tears for him who is moved by the sight of their flowing. But, had he known it, he would just the same have stayed; for man's pity is infinite.

CHAPTER VII

EVE TRIUMPHANT

" THERE ! " she said, after a few minutes. " The storm is over."

She raised her beautiful face, now lit with a smile :

" No black on my eye-lashes, you see," she added, gaily. " No rouge on my lips. . . . Take note, please. . . . Nothing that comes off ! "

This versatility of mood, the despair, which he had felt to be real, followed by a light-heartedness which he felt to be equally sincere; all this bewildered Philippe.

She began to laugh :

" Philippe ! Philippe ! You look as though you did not understand much about women . . . and even less about girls ! "

She rose and went to the next room, which was her bedroom, as he saw by the white curtains and the arrangement of the furniture; and she returned with an album, in which she showed him, on the first page, the photograph of a child, crying :

76

"Look, Philippe. I haven't changed. At two years old, just as now, I used to have great big sorrows and eyes that flowed like taps."

He turned the pages of the album. There were portraits of Suzanne at all ages: Suzanne as a child, Suzanne as a little girl, Suzanne as a young girl; and each was more bewitching than the last.

At the bottom of one page, he read:

"*Suzanne, twenty.*"

"Lord, how pretty you were!" he muttered, dazed by that image of beauty and gladness.

And he looked at Suzanne, in spite of himself.

"I have grown older," she said. "Three long years. . . ."

He shrugged his shoulders without replying, for, on the contrary, he thought her lovelier still; and he turned the pages. Two loose photographs slipped to the floor. She put out her hand to take them, but did not complete the movement.

"May I?" asked Philippe.

"Yes, certainly."

He was much astonished when he examined one of the portraits:

"This," he said, "makes you look older than you are. . . . How funny! And why that old-fashioned dress? . . . That quaint way of doing your hair. . . . It's you . . . and yet it's not you. . . . Who is it?"

" Mamma," she said.

He was surprised, knowing Jorancé's persistent rancour, that he should have given his daughter the portrait of a mother whom she had been taught to believe long dead. And he remembered the riotous adventures of the divorced wife, now the beautiful Mme. de Glaris, who was celebrated in the chronicles of fast society for her dresses and her jewellery and whose photographs were displayed in the shop-windows of the Rue de Rivoli for the admiration of the passers-by.

" Yes," he said, awkwardly and not quite knowing what he was saying, " yes, you are like her. . . . And is this also . . . ? "

He suppressed a movement of astonishment. This time, he clearly recognized Suzanne's mother, or rather the Mme. de Glaris of the Rue de Rivoli, bare-shouldered, decked in her pearls and diamonds, shameless and magnificent.

Suzanne, who kept her eyes raised to his face, did not speak; and they remained opposite each other, motionless and silent.

" Does she know the truth? " Philippe asked himself. " No . . . no . . . it's not possible. . . . She must have bought this photograph, because of the likeness to herself which she saw in it, and she does not suspect anything. . . ."

But he was not satisfied with his surmise and he dared not question the girl, for fear of touching upon one of those mysterious griefs which become more acute when once they are no longer secret.

She put the two portraits back in the album and locked the clasp with a little key. Then, after a long pause, laying her hand on Philippe's arm, she said to him, in words that corresponded strangely with the thoughts that troubled him:

"Do not be angry with me, dear, and, above all, do not judge me too severely. There is a Suzanne in me whom I do not know well . . . and who often frightens me. . . . She is capricious, jealous, wrong-headed, capable of anything . . . yes, of anything. . . . The real Suzanne is good and sensible: 'You're *my* daughter to-day,' papa used to say to me, when I was a little girl. And he said it in such a happy tone! But, the next day, I was his daughter no longer; and, struggle and fight as hard as I might, I could not become so again. . . . Things prevented me; and I used to cry because papa seemed to hate me. . . . And I wanted to be good. . . . And I still want to and I always do. . . . But there is nothing in the world so hard . . . because the other . . . the other one does not want to. . . . And besides . . ."

" What ? "

She waited a moment, as though hesitating, and continued:

" And, besides, what she wants, what the other Suzanne wants does not appear to me so very unreasonable. It is an immense longing to love somebody, but to love madly, boundlessly, to love too well. . . . Then it seems to me that life has no other object . . . and all the rest bores me. . . . You know, Philippe, even when I was ever so small, that word love used to upset me. And, later . . . and now, at certain times, I feel my brain going and all my soul seeking, waiting. . . ."

She hid her face again, as though seized with a sudden feeling of bashfulness, and Philippe saw, between her fingers, her crimson forehead and cheeks.

His pity swelled within him. Through those desultory confidences, he saw Suzanne as she was, ignorant, ill-informed about herself and about the realities of life, troubled with desires which she took for unsatisfied feelings, torn by the implacable duel between contrary instincts and possessing nothing to counteract her woman's nature but a wayward and melancholy virtue.

How good it would be to save her! He went up to her and, very gently, said:

" You must get married, Suzanne."

She shook her head:

"There have been young men here who seemed to like me, but they always went away after a few days. One would almost think that they were afraid of me . . . or that they had heard things . . . against me. . . . Besides . . . I didn't care for them. . . . It was not they . . . that I was waiting for. . . . It was somebody else. . . . And he did not come."

He understood the irreparable words which she was about to utter and he ardently hoped that she would not utter them.

Suzanne guessed his wish and was silent. But the avowal was so clear, even when unexpressed, that Philippe read all its passion in the long silence that followed. And Suzanne experienced a great joy, as though the indissoluble bond of words were linking them together. She added:

"It was a little your fault, Philippe, and you felt it, in a way, at dinner. Yes, a little your fault. . . . In Paris, I lived a dangerous life beside you. . . . Just think, we were always together, always by ourselves, we two; and, for days at a time, I had the right to think that there was no one in the world but you and I. It was for me that you talked, it was to make me worthy of yourself that you explained things to me which I did not know, that you took me to see the beautiful sights in

the churches, in the old towns. . . . And I, I was
amazed. At what I was learning? Oh, no, Philippe, but at the new world that suddenly opened
up to me. I did not listen to your words, but I
listened to the sound of your voice. My eyes saw
only your eyes. It was your admiration that I
admired; your love for. the beautiful was what I
loved. All that you taught me to know . . . and
to love, Philippe, was . . . yourself."

Notwithstanding his inward rebellion, the words
entered into Philippe's being like a caress; and he
too almost forgot himself in the pleasure of listening to the sound of a soft voice and looking into
eyes that are dear to one.

He said, simply:

" And Marthe? "

She did not answer; and he felt that, like many
women, she was indifferent to considerations of
that sort. To them, love is a reason that excuses
everything.

Then, seeking to create a diversion, he repeated:

" You must get married, Suzanne, you must.
That is where your safety lies."

" Oh, I know! " she said, wringing her hands in
despair. " I know . . . only . . ."

" Only what? "

" I haven't the strength to."

" You must find the strength."

" I can't. . . . I ought to have it given me. I
ought to have . . . oh, nothing very much, perhaps . . . a little gladness . . . a glad memory
. . . the thought that my life will not have been
entirely wasted. . . . The thought that I too shall
have had my spell of love. . . . But that short spell
I ask for . . . I beg for it, I pray for it."

He blurted out:

" You will find it in marriage, Suzanne."

" No, no," she said, more bitterly, " only the man
I love can give it to me. . . . I want, once at least,
to feel a pair of arms around me, nothing but that,
I assure you . . . to lay my head on your shoulder
and to remain like that, for an instant."

She was so near to Philippe that the muslin of
her bodice touched his clothes and he breathed the
scent of her hair. He felt a mad temptation to
take her in his arms. And it would have been a
very small thing, as she had said: one of those moments of happiness which one plucks like a flower
and remembers.

She looked at him, not sadly now, nor resigned,
but smiling, archly, with all the ingenious charm of
the woman who is trying to conquer.

He turned pale and murmured:

" Suzanne, I am your friend. Be my friend,
simply, and let your imagination . . ."

" You're afraid," she said.

He tried to jest:

"Afraid! Goodness gracious me, of what?"

"Afraid of the one little affectionate action which I ask of you, the action of a brother kissing his sister. That's what you shrink from, Philippe."

"I shrink from it because it is wrong and wicked," he declared, firmly. "That is the only reason."

"No, Philippe, there is another reason."

"Which is that?"

"You love me."

"I! I love you? . . . I!"

"Yes, you, Philippe, you love me. And I defy you to look me in the face, to look me straight in the eyes and deny it."

And, without giving him time to recover, she continued, bending over him eagerly:

"You were in love with me, before I fell in love with you. It was your love that created mine. Don't protest, you have no right to do so now, for *you know.* . . . And I, I knew it from the first day. Oh, believe me, a woman is never mistaken. . . . Your eyes, when they looked at me, had a new look in them . . . there, the look of just now. You have never looked like that at any woman, Philippe; not even at Marthe, . . . no . . . not even at her. . . . You never loved her, her nor the others. I was the first. Love was a thing

unknown to you and you do not understand it yet
. . . and you sit there in front of me, nonplussed
and dumbfoundered, because the truth appears to
you and because you love me, Philippe, because you
love me, my dear Philippe. . . ."

She clung to him, in an upheaval of hope and
certainty, and he seemed not to resist.

"You were afraid, Philippe. That is why you
made up your mind not to see me again. . . . That
is why you spoke so harshly to me just now. . . .
You were afraid, because you love me. . . . Do
you understand now? . . . Oh, Philippe, I should
not have acted with you as I have done, if you did
not love me. . . . I should never have had the pre-
sumption! . . . But I knew. . . . I knew . . . and
you don't deny it, do you? . . . Oh, how I suffered! My jealousy of Marthe! . . . To-day
again, when she kissed you. . . . And the thought
of going away without as much as saying good-
bye to you! . . . And the thought of that marriage! . . . What a torture! . . . But it's over
now, is it not? I shall suffer no more . . . because
you love me."

She spoke these last words with a sort of timor-
ous hesitation and without taking her eyes from
Philippe's face, as though expecting him to give
an answer that would calm the sudden anguish with
which she was torn.

He was silent. His eyes were dull, his forehead creased with wrinkles. He seemed to be reflecting and did not appear to reck that Suzanne
was there so close to him, her arms clinging to his
arms.

She whispered:

" Philippe. . . . Philippe. . . ."

Had he heard? He remained impassive. Then,
little by little, Suzanne released her embrace. Her
hands fell to her sides. She gazed with infinite
distress upon the man she loved and, suddenly, sank
into a heap, weeping:

" Oh, I am mad! . . . I am mad! Why did I
speak? "

It was a horrible ordeal for her, after the hope
that had excited her, and this time it was real tears
that flowed down her cheeks. The sound of the
sobs roused Philippe from his dream. He listened
to it sadly and then began to pace the room. Moved
though he was, what was passing within him
troubled him even more. He loved Suzanne!

It did not for a second occur to him to deny the
truth. From the first sentences that Suzanne had
spoken and without his having to seek for further
proofs, he had admitted his love even as one admits
the presence of a thing that one sees and touches.
And that was why Suzanne, at the mere sight of
Philippe's attitude, had suddenly realized the im-

prudence which she had committed in speaking:
Philippe, once warned, was escaping her. He was
one of those men who become conscious of their
duty at the very moment when they perceive their
fault.

"Philippe!" she said, once more. "Philippe!"
. As he did not reply, she took his hand again and
whispered:

"You love me, though . . . you love me. . . .
Well, then, if you love me . . ."

The tears did not disfigure her exquisite face.
On the contrary, grief decked her with a new,
graver and more touching beauty. And she ended,
ingenuously enough:

"Then, if you love me, why do you repel me?
Surely, when one loves, one does not repel the
thing one loves. . . . And you love me. . . ."

The pretty mouth was all entreaty. Philippe observed its voluptuous action. It was as though the
two lips delighted in uttering words of love and as
though they could pronounce no others.

He turned away his eyes to escape the fascina-
tion and, controlling himself, mastering his voice
so that she might not perceive its tremor, he
said:

"It is just because I love you, Suzanne, that I
am repulsing you . . . because I love you too
well. . . ."

The phrase implied a breach which she felt to be irreparable. She did not attempt to protest. It was finished. And she knew this so thoroughly that, a moment later, when Philippe opened the door and prepared to go away, she did not even raise her head.

He did not go, however, for fear of offending her. He sat down. There was only a little table between them. But how far he was from her! And how it must surprise her that all her feminine wiles, her coquetry, the allurement of her lips were powerless to subjugate the will of that man who loved her!

The belfry-clock struck ten. When Morestal and Jorancé arrived, Suzanne and Philippe had not exchanged a single word.

*
* *

"Ready to start, Philippe?" cried Morestal. "Have you said good-bye to Suzanne?"

She replied:

"Yes, we have said good-bye."

"Well, then it's my turn," he said, kissing her. "Jorancé, it's settled that you're coming with us."

"As far as the Butte-aux-Loups."

"If you go as far as the Butte," said Suzanne to her father, "you may just as well go on to the Old Mill and come back by the high-road."

"That's true. But are you staying behind, Suzanne?"

She decided to see them out of Saint-Élophe.
She quickly wrapped a silk scarf round her head:

"Here I am," she said.

The four of them walked off, along the sleeping
streets of the little town, and Morestal at once
began to comment on his interview with Captain
Daspry. A very intelligent man, the captain, who
had not failed to see the importance of the Old
Mill as a block-house, to use his expression. But,
from another point of view, he had given something of a shock to Morestal's opinions on the attitude which a French officer should maintain towards his inferiors.

"Just imagine, Philippe: he refuses to punish
the soldiers I told him about . . . you know, the
pillagers whom Saboureux complained of. . . .
Well, he refuses to punish them . . . even the
leader of the band, one Duvauchel, a lover of every
country but his own, who glories in his ideas, they
say. Can you understand it? The rascal escapes
with a fine of ten francs, an apology, a promise not
to do it again and a lecture from his captain! And
Mossieu Daspry pretends that, with kindness and
patience, he succeeds in turning Duvauchel and fellows of his kidney into his best soldiers! What
humbug! As though there were any way of

taming those beggars, short of discipline! A pack of good-for-nothing scoundrels, who would fly across the frontier the moment the first shot was fired!"

Philippe had instinctively slackened his pace. Suzanne was walking beside him; and, every now and then, by the light of an electric lamp, he saw the golden halo of her hair and the delicate profile draped in the silk scarf.

He felt full of gentleness for her, now that he no longer feared her, and he was tempted to speak kind words to her, as to a little sister of whom one is very fond. But the silence was sweeter still and he did not wish to break its charm.

They passed the last houses. The street ran into a white country-road, lined with tall poplars. And they heard scraps of Morestal's conversation:

"Oh, yes! Captain Daspry! Leniency, friendly relations between superiors and inferiors, the barracks looked upon as a school of brotherhood, with the officers for instructors! That's all very well; but do you know what a system of that sort leads to? An army of deserters and renegades. . . ."

Suzanne said, in a low voice:

"May I have your arm, Philippe?"

He at once slipped his arm through hers, happy at the thought of pleasing her. And he felt, besides, a great relief at seeing that she leant against

him with the confidence of a friend. They were
going to part and nothing would tarnish the pure
memory of that day. It was a comforting impression, which nevertheless caused him a certain sad-
ness. Duty fulfilled always leaves a taste of bitterness behind. The intoxication of sacrifice no longer
stimulates you; and you begin to understand what
you have refused.

In the warm night, amid all the perfumes that
stirred in the breeze, Suzanne's own scent was
wafted up to him. He inhaled it long and greedily
and reflected that no scent had ever excited him
before:

" Good-bye," he said, within himself. " Good-
bye, little girl; good-bye to what was my love."

And, during those last minutes, as though he
were granting a crowning grace to his impossible
longings and his forbidden dreams, he yielded to
the delights of that love which had blossomed so
mysteriously in the unknown regions of his soul.

" Good-bye," Suzanne now said. " Good-bye,
Philippe."

" Are you going? "

" Yes, or else my father would come back with
me; and I want nobody ... nobody...."

Jorancé and old Morestal had stopped near a
bench, at a place where two paths met, the wider
of which, the one on the left, climbed up towards

the frontier. The spot was known as the Carrefour du Grand Chêne, or Great Oak Crossways.

Morestal kissed the girl again:

" Good-bye, for the present, Suzanne. And don't forget that I'm coming to your wedding."

He pressed the spring of his repeater:

" I say, Philippe, it's a quarter past ten. . . . True, there's no hurry. . . . Your mother and Marthe must be asleep by now. No matter, let's get on. . . ."

" Look here, father, if you don't mind, I would rather take the direct road. . . . The path by the Butte-aux-Loups is longer; and I am feeling rather tired."

In reality, like Suzanne, Philippe wanted to go home alone, so that nothing might disturb the melancholy charm of his dream. Old Morestal's long speeches terrified him.

" As you please, my boy," cried the old man. " But mind you don't put up the bolt or the chain on the hall-door."

Jorancé impressed the same injunctions on Suzanne and the two walked away.

" Good-bye, Philippe," said the girl, once again.

He had already entered the path on the right.

" Good-bye, Suzanne," he said.

" Give me your hand, Philippe."

For his hand to reach Suzanne's, he had to turn

two or three steps back. He hesitated. But she had come towards him and, very gently, drew him to the foot of the path:

"Philippe, we must not part like this. . . . It is too sad! Let us go back together to Saint-Élophe . . . as far as the house. . . . Please do. . . ."

"No," he said, curtly.

"Oh!" she moaned. "I asked so that I might be with you a little longer. . . . It is so sad! But you are right. Let us part."

He said, in a kinder tone:

"Suzanne. . . . Suzanne. . . ."

Bending her head a little, she put out her forehead to him:

"Kiss me, Philippe."

He stooped, intending to kiss the curls of her hair. But she gave a swift movement and flung her arms round his neck.

He felt that he was lost and made a despairing effort. Suzanne's lips were close to his, offering themselves.

"Oh, Suzanne . . . Suzanne, my darling . . ." he whispered, abandoning all resistance and pressing the girl to his breast. . . .

CHAPTER VIII

THE TRAP

THE road which Morestal and his friend followed first makes a bend and climbs the wooded side of a ravine. It was formerly used for foresting purposes and is still paved with large stones which are covered with mud after a rainy day and make the ascent slippery and difficult.

Morestal was panting for breath when he reached the top:

"We ought . . ." he said, "to see . . . Philippe from here."

Faint clouds dimmed the light of the moon, but still, at certain places denuded of trees, they were able to distinguish the other side of the ravine.

He called out:

"Hullo! . . . Philippe!"

"I tell you what," said Jorancé. "I expect Philippe did not like to let Suzanne go home alone and he is taking her back, at any rate as far as the houses."

"I dare say," said Morestal. "Poor Suzanne,

94

she doesn't look very bright. So you've made up
your mind to get her married?"

"Yes . . . I'm getting her married . . . it's all
settled."

They started walking again, and, by an imperceptible slope, came to two large trees, after which
the road turned to the right. From that point on-
wards, running through pine-woods along the line
of the ridges, it marked the frontier as far as the
Col du Diable.

On their left was the German slope, which was
steeper.

"Yes," repeated Jorancé, "it's all settled. Of
course, Suzanne might have met a younger man
. . . a better-looking man . . . but no one more
respectable or more serious. . . . To say nothing
of his having a very firm character; and, with Suzanne, a certain amount of firmness is necessary.
Besides . . ."

"Yes?" said Morestal, perceiving his hesitation.

"Well, you see, Morestal, Suzanne has got to
be married. She inherits from me an upright nature and strict principles . . . but she is not only
my daughter . . . and sometimes I am afraid of
finding . . . bad instincts in her."

"Have you discovered anything?"

"Oh, no! And I am sure that there is nothing
to discover. But it's the future I'm afraid of.

One day or another, she may know temptation . . .
some one may make love to her . . . turn her head
with fair words. When that time comes, will she
know how to resist? Oh, Morestal, the thought of
it drives me mad! I couldn't bear it. . . . Just
think, the daughter, following after the mother.
. . . Oh, I believe . . . I believe I should kill
her! . . ."

Morestal jested:

" What a fuss about nothing! A good little girl
like Suzanne! . . ."

" Yes, you are right, it's absurd. But I can't
help it, I can't forget. . . . And I don't want to,
either. My duty is to think of everything and to
give her a guide, a master who will advise her.
. . . I know Suzanne: she will make a perfect
wife. . . ."

" And she will have lots of children; and they
will be very happy," Morestal wound up. " Come,
you're boring me and boring yourself with your
fancies. . . . Let's talk of something else. By the
way . . ."

He waited for Jorancé to come up with him.
The two walked on abreast. And Morestal, who
was interested in no subject outside his personal
prejudice, resumed:

" By the way, can you tell me — if it's not a professional secret, of course — can you tell me who that man Dourlowski is exactly?"

"Six months ago," replied Jorancé, "I should not have been able to answer your question. But now . . ."

"But now? . . ."

"He is no longer in our service."

"Do you think he has gone over to the other side?"

"I expect so, but I haven't the least proof of it. In any case, there's not much to be said in the fellow's favour. Why do you ask? Have you anything to do with him?"

"No, no," said Morestal, remaining thoughtful.

They went on in silence. The wind, which blew more strongly on the ridge, played among the trees. The pine-needles crackled under the soles of their boots. The moon had disappeared, but the sky was white with light.

"The Pierre-Branlante. . . . The Cheminée-des-Fées," said Morestal, pointing to the vaguely-seen shapes of two huge boulders known by those names of the Rocking Stone and the Fairies' Chimney.

They walked for another moment:

"Eh? What is it?" said Jorancé, feeling his companion catch him by the arm.

" Did you hear? "

" No."

" Listen ! "

" Well, what? "

" Didn't you hear a sort of a hoot? "

" Yes, the hoot of an owl."

" Are you sure? It doesn't sound natural to me."

" What do you say it is, then? A signal? "

" I'm certain of it."

Jorancé reflected:

" After all, it's quite possible . . . some smug-
gler perhaps. . . . But it's a bad moment to have
chosen."

" Why? "

" Well, now that the German post has been cut
down, it's likely that all this part of the frontier is
being more closely watched than usual."

" Yes, of course," said Morestal. " Still, that
owl's hoot . . ."

There was a short slope and then they emerged
upon a higher upland, surrounded by enormous fir-
trees, which formed a sort of rampart. This was
the Butte-aux-Loups. The road cut it in two;
and the posts of each country stood facing each
other.

Jorancé noticed that the German post had been
put up again, but in a makeshift fashion, with the

aid of a number of large stones which kept it in position.

"A gust of wind and down it comes again," he said, shaking it.

"I say, mind what you're about!" said Morestal, with a chuckle. "Don't you see yourself toppling it over and having the police down upon you? . . . You'd better make a strategic movement to the rear, my friend! . . ."

But he had not finished speaking when another cry reached his ears.

"Ah, this time," said Morestal, "you'll admit. . . ."

"Yes . . . yes . . ." Jorancé agreed. "An owl gives a duller, slower hoot. . . . It really is like a signal, a hundred yards or so ahead of us. . . . Smugglers, of course, French or German."

"Suppose we turned back?" said Morestal. "Aren't you afraid of being mixed up in an affair? . . ."

"Why? It's the custom-house people's business; it doesn't concern you and me. They can settle it among themselves. . . ."

They listened for a moment and then went on, thoughtfully, with watchful ears.

After the Butte-aux-Loups, the ridge becomes flatter, the forest spreads out and the road, now freer, winds among the trees, runs from one slope to the other, avoids the big roots, passes round the inequalities of the ground and, at times, disappears from sight under a bed of dead leaves.

But the moon had come out again and Morestal walked straight in front of him, without hesitation. He knew the frontier so well! He could have followed it with his eyes closed, in the dusk of the darkest night! At one place, there was a branch that blocked the way; at another, there was the trunk of an old oak which sounded hollow when he hit it with his stick. And he announced the branch before he came to it; and he struck at the old oak.

His uneasiness, which began to seem unreasonable, was dispelled. Consulting his watch again, he hurried his steps, so as to reach home by the time which he had said.

But suddenly he stopped. He thought he saw a shadow hiding, thirty or forty yards away from him:

" Did you see? " he whispered.

" Yes . . . I saw. . . ."

And, all at once, there came a shrill, strident whistle, apparently from the very place where the shadow had vanished.

" Don't move," said Jorancé.

They waited, their hearts tense with the anguish of what was coming.

A minute passed and more minutes; and then there was a sound of footsteps, below them, on the German side, the sound of a man hurrying. . . .

Morestal thought of the precipitous hill which he had described to Dourlowski as the way up to the frontier from the Albern Woods, by the Cold Spring, the Fontaine-Froide. In all certainty, somebody was scaling the upper portion of that precipice, clinging on to the branches and dragging himself along the pebbles.

"A deserter!" whispered Jorancé. "No nonsense now!"

But Morestal pushed him away and began to run to where the two roads crossed. At the very moment when he reached the spot, a man appeared, all frenzied and out of breath, and stammered, in French:

"Save me! . . . I've been given away! . . . I'm frightened! . . ."

Morestal seized hold of him and flung him off the road:

"Run! . . . Look sharp! . . . Straight ahead of you!"

There was the report of a rifle. The man staggered, with a moan; but he was evidently only wounded, for, after a few seconds, he drew himself up and made off through the woods.

A chase ensued forthwith. Four or five Germans crossed the frontier and set off in pursuit of the fugitive, swearing as they went, while their comrades, forming the greater number, turned towards Morestal.

Jorancé took him round the waist and compelled him to recoil:

" This way," he said, " over there. . . . They won't dare . . ."

They returned in the direction of the Butte-aux-Loups, but were at once caught up:

" Halt!" commanded a rough voice. " I arrest you. . . . You are accomplices. . . . I arrest you."

" We are in France," retorted Jorancé, facing his aggressors.

A hand fell on his shoulder:

" We'll see about that. . . . We'll see about that. . . . You're coming with us."

The men surrounded them; but, vigorous both and exasperated, they succeeded in fighting their way through with their fists:

" To the Butte-aux-Loups," said Jorancé, " and keep to the left of the road."

" We're not on the left," said Morestal, who saw,

after a moment, that they had branched off to the right.

They re-entered French territory; but the police who were pursuing the deserter, having lost his tracks, now fell back in their direction.

Thereupon they made a bend to the right, hesitated for a moment, careful not to cross the road, and then set off again; and, still tracked by the men, whom they felt close upon their heels, they reached the acclivity of the Butte-aux-Loups. At that moment, surrounded on all hands and utterly blown, they had to stop to take breath.

"Arrest them!" said the leader of the men, in whom they recognized the German commissary, Weisslicht. "Arrest them! We are in Germany."

"You lie!" roared Morestal, fighting with wild energy. "You have not the right. . . . It's a dirty trap!"

It was a violent struggle, but did not last long. He received a blow on the chin with the butt of a rifle, reeled, but continued to defend himself, hitting and biting his adversaries. At last, they succeeded in throwing him and, to stifle his shouting, they gagged him.

Jorancé, who had taken a leap to the rear and was standing with his back to a tree, resisted, protesting:

"I am M. Jorancé, special commissary at Saint-Élophe. I am on my own ground here. We are in France. There's the frontier."

The men flung themselves upon him and dragged him away, while he shouted at the top of his voice:

"Help! Help! They're arresting the French commissary on French soil!"

A report was heard, followed by another. Morestal, with a superhuman effort, had knocked down the policeman who held him and once more took to flight, with a cord cutting into one of his wrists and with a gag in his mouth.

But, two hundred yards further, as he was turning towards the Col du Diable, his foot knocked against the root of a tree and he fell.

He was at once overtaken and firmly bound.

A few moments later, the two prisoners were carried by the police to the road leading through the Albern Woods and hoisted on the backs of a couple of horses. They were taken to the Col du Diable and, from there, past the Wildermann factory and the hamlet of Torins, sent on to the German town of Börsweilen.

PART II

CHAPTER I

THE TWO WOMEN

Suzanne Jorancé pushed the swing-gate and entered the grounds of the Old Mill.

She was dressed in white and her face looked fresh and cool under a large hat of Leghorn straw, with its black-velvet strings hanging loose upon her shoulders. Her short skirt showed her dainty ankles. She walked with a brisk step, using a tall, iron-shod stick, while her disengaged hand crumpled some flowers which she had gathered on the way and which she dropped heedlessly as she went.

The Morestals' peaceful house was waking in the morning sun. Several of the windows were open; and Suzanne saw Marthe writing at the table in her bedroom.

She called out:

" Can I come up? "

But Mme. Morestal appeared at one of the windows of the drawing-room and made an imperious sign to her:

" Hush! Don't speak!"

" What's the matter?" asked Suzanne, when she joined the old lady.

" They're asleep."

" Who?"

" Why, the father and son."

" Oh!" said Suzanne. " Philippe too? . . ."

" Yes, they must have come in late and they are resting. Neither of them has rung his bell yet. But tell me, Suzanne, aren't you going away?"

" To-morrow . . . or the next day. . . . I confess, I'm in no hurry to go."

Mme. Morestal took her to her daughter-in-law's room and asked:

" Philippe's still asleep, isn't he?"

" I suppose so," said Marthe. " I haven't heard him move. . . ."

" Nor I Morestal. . . . And yet he's an early riser, as a rule. . . . And Philippe, who wanted to go tramping at daybreak! . . . However, so much the better, sleep suits both of my men. . . . By the way, Marthe, didn't the shooting wake you in the night?"

" The shooting!"

" Oh, of course, your room is on the other side. The sound came from the frontier. . . . Some poacher, I suppose. . . ."

" Were M. Morestal and Philippe in?"

" Surely! It must have been one or two o'clock
. . . perhaps later . . . I don't quite know."

She put the tea-pot and the jar of honey, which
Marthe had had for breakfast, on the tray; and, with
her mania for tidying, obeying some mysterious
principle of symmetry, settled her daughter-in-law's
things and any piece of furniture in the room that
had been moved from its place. This done, with
her hands hanging before her, she looked round for
an excuse to discontinue this irksome activity.
Then, discovering none, she left the room.

" How early you are," said Marthe to Suzanne.

" I wanted air . . . and movement. . . . Besides, I told Philippe that I would come and fetch
him. I want to go and see the ruins of the Petite-
Chartreuse with him . . . It's a bore that he's not
up yet."

She seemed disappointed at this accident which
deprived her of a pleasure.

" Do you mind if I finish my letters?" asked
Marthe, taking up her pen.

Suzanne strolled round the room, looking out of
the window, leant to see if Philippe's was open,
then sat down opposite Marthe and examined her
long and carefully. She noted the eye-lids, which
were a little rumpled; the uneven colouring; the
tiny wrinkles on the temples; a few white hairs
mingling with the dark tresses; all that proclaims

time's little victories over waning youth. And, raising her eyes, she saw herself in a glass.

Marthe surprised her glance and cried, with an admiration free from all envy:

"You are splendid, Suzanne! You look like a triumphant goddess. What triumph have you achieved?"

Suzanne flushed and, in her confusion, said, at random:

"But you, Marthe, you look worried. . . ."

"Well, yes . . . perhaps I am."

And Marthe told how, on the previous evening, finding herself alone with her mother-in-law, she had spoken to her of Philippe's new ideas, the spirit of his work, his plan of resigning his position and his firm intention to have an explanation with M. Morestal.

"Well?"

"Well," said Marthe, "my mother-in-law flew out. She absolutely objects to any explanation whatever."

"Why?"

"M. Morestal is suffering from heart-trouble. Dr. Borel, who has attended him for the last twenty years, says that he must be spared any annoyance, any excessive excitement. And an interview with Philippe might have fatal results. . . . What can one reply to that?"

" You will have to tell Philippe."

" Certainly.   And he, he must either keep silent and continue to lead an intolerable existence, or else, at the cost of the most terrible anguish, face M. Morestal's anger."

She was silent for a moment and then, striking the table with her clenched fists:

" Oh," she exclaimed, " if I could only take all those worries upon myself and save Philippe's peace of mind!"

Suzanne felt all the force of her vehemence and energy.   No pain would have frightened Marthe, no sacrifice would have been beyond her strength.

" Do you love Philippe very much?" she asked.

Marthe smiled:

" With all my heart. . . . He deserves it."

The younger woman felt a certain bitterness and could not help saying:

" Does he love you as much as you love him?"

" Why, yes, I think so. . . . I deserve it too."

" And do you trust him?"

" Oh, fully!   Philippe is the most loyal creature I know."

" Still . . ."

" What?"

" Nothing."

" Yes, say what you were going to. . . . Oh, you need not be afraid of asking me questions!"

"Well, I was thinking . . . suppose Philippe loved another woman. . . ."

Marthe burst out laughing:

"If you knew how little importance Philippe attaches to all that business of love!"

"However, supposing . . ."

"Very well, supposing," she said, pretending to be serious. "Philippe loves another woman. He is madly in love with her. What then?"

"In that case, what would you do?"

"Upon my word . . . I've never thought about it."

"Wouldn't you go for a divorce?"

"And my children?"

"But, if he wanted to be divorced?"

"Then it would be, 'Good-bye, M. Philippe!'"

Suzanne reflected, without taking her eyes from Marthe, as though she were spying for a sign of uneasiness on her features or seeking to fathom the depths of her most secret thoughts.

She murmured:

"And, if he deceived you?"

This time, the thrust went home. Marthe shivered, stung to the quick. Her face altered. And she said, in a voice which she made an effort to contain:

"Oh, that, no! If Philippe fell in love with another woman, if he wanted to begin his life again, without me, and if he confessed it frankly, I should consent to everything . . . yes, to everything, even to a divorce, however great my despair. . . . But treachery, lying . . ."

" You would not forgive him? "

" Never! Philippe is not a man whom one can forgive. He is a conscious man, who knows what he is doing, incapable of a weakness; and no forgiveness would absolve him. Besides, I myself could not . . . no . . . I could not indeed." And she added, " I have too much pride."

The phrase was gravely and simply uttered and revealed a haughtiness of soul which Suzanne had not suspected. She felt a sort of confusion in the presence of the rival whom she was attacking and who held her at bay with such disdain.

A long silence divided the two women; and Marthe said:

" You're in one of your wicked moods to-day, Suzanne, aren't you? "

" I am too happy to be wicked," chuckled the girl. " Only it's such a strange happiness! I am afraid it won't last."

" Your marriage . . ."

" I won't get married! " declared Suzanne, excitedly. " I won't get married at any price! I hate that man. . . . He's not the only man in the world, is he? There are others . . . others who will love

me. . . . I too am worthy of being loved . . .
worthy of being lived for! . . ."

There were tears in her voice; and so great a
despondency overwhelmed her features that Marthe
felt a longing to console her, as was her habit
in such cases. Nevertheless, she said nothing.
Suzanne had wounded her, not so much by her
questions as by her attitude, by a certain sarcasm
in her accent and by an air of defiance that mingled
with the expression of her grief.

She preferred to cut short a painful scene the
meaning of which escaped her, although the scene
itself did not astonish her on Suzanne's part:

"I am going downstairs," she said. "It's time
for the post; and I am expecting letters."

"So you're leaving me!" said Suzanne, in a
broken voice.

Marthe could not help laughing:

"Well, yes, I am leaving you in this room . . .
unless you refuse to stay. . . ."

Suzanne ran after her and, holding her back:

"You mustn't! I only ask for a movement, a
kind word. . . . I am passing through a terrible
time, I need help and you . . . you repel me. . . .
It's you who are repelling me, don't forget that.
. . . It's you. . . ."

"That's understood," said Marthe. "I am a
cruel friend. . . . Only, you see, my dear little

Suzanne, if the thought of your marriage upsets you to that extent, it might be a good plan to tell your father. . . . Come, come along downstairs and calm yourself."

They found Mme. Morestal below, feather-broom in hand, an apron tied round her waist, waging her daily battle against a dust that existed only in her imagination.

"I suppose you know, mamma, that Philippe is not yet up?"

"The lazy fellow! It's nearly nine o'clock. I hope he's not ill!"

"Oh, no!" said Marthe. "But, all the same, when I go up again, I'll look in and see."

Mme. Morestal went as far as the hall with the two young women. Suzanne was already walking away, without a word, with the face which she wore on her black days, as Marthe said, when Mme. Morestal called her back:

"You're forgetting your stick, child."

The old lady had taken the long, iron-shod walking-stick from the umbrella-stand. But, suddenly, she began to rummage among the canes and sunshades, muttering:

"Well, that's funny. . . ."

"What's the matter?" asked Marthe.

"I can't find Morestal's stick. And yet it's always here."

" He must have put it down somewhere else."

" Impossible! If so, it would be the first time in his life. I know him so well! . . . What can it mean? . . . Victor!"

The man ran into the hall:

" Yes, ma'am?"

" Victor, why isn't your master's cane here?"

" I have a notion, ma'am, that the master has gone out."

" Gone out! But you ought to have told me. . . . I was beginning to be anxious."

" I said so just now to Catherine."

" But what makes you think . . . ?"

" In the first place, the master did not put his boots outside his door as usual. . . . M. Philippe neither. . . ."

" What!" said Marthe. " Has M. Philippe gone out too?"

" Very early this morning, ma'am . . . before my time for getting up."

In spite of herself, Suzanne Jorancé protested:

" But no, it's not conceivable. . . ."

" Why, when I came down," said Victor, " the front-door was not locked."

" And your master never forgets to turn the key, does he?"

" Never. As the door was not locked, it means

either that the master has gone out . . . or
else. . . ."

" Or else what?"

" That he hasn't come in. . . . Only, I say that
as I might say anything that came into my
head. . . ."

" Not come in!" exclaimed Mme. Morestal.

She reflected for a second, then turned on her
heels, ran up the stairs with surprising agility,
crossed a passage and entered her husband's bedroom.

She uttered a cry and called:

" Marthe! . . . Marthe! . . ."

But the young woman, who had followed her,
was already on her way to the second floor, with
Suzanne.

Philippe's room was at the back.   She opened the
door quickly and stood on the threshold, speechless.

Philippe was not there; and the bed had not even
been undone.

CHAPTER II

THE three women met in the drawing-room. Mme. Morestal walked up and down in dismay, hardly knowing what she was saying:

"Not in! . . . Philippe neither! . . . Victor, you must run . . . but where to? . . . Where is he to look? . . . Oh, it's really too terrible! . . ."

She suddenly stepped in front of Marthe and stammered:

"The . . . the shots . . . last night. . . ."

Marthe, pale with anxiety, did not reply. She had had the same awful thought from the first moment.

But Suzanne exclaimed:

"In any case, Marthe, you need not be alarmed. Philippe did not take the road by the frontier."

"Are you sure?"

"We separated at the Carrefour du Grand-Chêne. M. Morestal and papa went on by themselves. Philippe came straight back."

"No, he can't have come straight back, or he would be here now," said Marthe. "What can he

have been doing all night? He has not even set
foot in his room!"

But Mme. Morestal was terrified by what Suzanne
had said. She could now no longer doubt that her
husband had taken the frontier-road; and the shots
had come from the frontier!

"Yes, that's true," said Suzanne, "but it was
only ten o'clock when we started from Saint-Élophe
and the shots which you heard were fired at one or
two o'clock in the morning. . . . You said so yourself."

"How can I tell?" cried the old lady, who was
beginning to lose her head entirely. "It may have
been much earlier."

"But your father must know," said Marthe to
Suzanne. "Did he tell you nothing?"

"I have not seen my father this morning," said
Suzanne. "He was not awake . . ."

She had not time to finish her sentence before
an idea burst in upon her, an idea so natural that
the two other women were struck by it also and
none of them dared put it into words.

Suzanne flew to the door, but Marthe held her
back. Why not telephone to Saint-Élophe, to the
special commissary's house?

A minute later, M. Jorancé's servant replied that
she had just noticed that her master was not in.
His bed had not been touched either.

"Oh!" said Suzanne, trembling all over. "My poor father! . . . Can anything have happened to him? . . . My poor father! I ought to have . . ."

· They stood for a moment as though paralyzed, all three, and incapable of taking a resolution. The man-servant went out saying that he would saddle the horse and gallop to the Col du Diable.

Marthe, who was nearest to the telephone, rang up the mayor's office at Saint-Élophe, on the off-chance, and asked for news. They knew nothing there. But two gendarmes, it seemed, had just crossed the square at a great pace. Thereupon, at the suggestion of Mme. Morestal, who had taken up the second receiver, she asked to be put on to the gendarmery. As soon as she was connected, she explained her reason for telephoning and was informed that the sergeant was on his way to the frontier with a peasant who declared that he had found the body of a man in the woods between the Butte-aux-Loups and the Col du Diable. That was all they were able to tell her. . . .

Mme. Morestal let go the receiver and fell in a dead faint. Marthe and Suzanne tried to attend to her. But their hands trembled and, when Catherine, the maid-servant, appeared upon the scene, they both ran out of the room, roused by a sudden energy and an immense need of doing something, of walking, of laying eyes upon that dead body whose blood-stained image obsessed their minds.

They went down the stairs of the terrace and scurried in the direction of the Étang-des-Moines. They had not gone fifty yards, when they were passed by Victor, who galloped by on horseback and shouted:

"Go in, go in! What's the use? I shall be back again!"

They went on nevertheless. But two roads offered: Suzanne wanted to take the one leading to the pass, on the left; Marthe, the one on the right, through the woods. They exchanged sharp words, blocking each other's way.

Suddenly, Suzanne, without knowing what she was saying, flung herself into her friend's arms, blurting out:

"I must tell you. . . . It is my duty. . . . Besides, it is all my fault. . . ."

Marthe, enraged and not understanding the words, which she was to remember so clearly later, spoke to her roughly:

"You're quite mad to-day," she said. "Leave me alone, do."

She darted into the woods and, in a few minutes, came to an abandoned quarry. The path went no further. She had a fit of fury, was on the verge of throwing herself on the ground and bursting into

tears and then retraced her steps, for she thought
she heard some one call.   It was Suzanne, who had
seen a man coming from the frontier on horseback
and who had vainly tried to make herself heard.
He was no doubt bringing news. . . .

Panting and exhausted, they went back again.
But there was no one at the Old Mill, no one but
Mme. Morestal and Catherine, who were praying
on the terrace.   All the servants had gone off, without plan or purpose, in search of information; and
the man on the horse, a peasant, had passed without
looking up.

Then they dropped on a bench near the balustrade and sat stupefied, worn out by the effort which
they had just made; and horrible minutes followed.
Each of the three women thought of her own special
sorrow and each, besides, suffered the anguish of
the unknown disaster that threatened all three of
them.   They dared not look at one another.   They
dared not speak, although the silence tortured them.
The least sound represented a source of foolish hope
or horrid dread; and, with their eyes fixed on the
line of dark woods, they waited.

Suddenly, they rose with a start.   Catherine, who
was keeping a look-out on the steps of the staircase,
had sprung to her feet:

" There's Henriot! " she cried.

" Henriot? " echoed Mme. Morestal.

" Yes, the gardener's boy: I can make him out from here."

" Where? We haven't seen him come."

" He must have taken a short cut. . . . He is coming up the stairs. . . . Quick, Henriot! . . . Hurry! . . . Do you know anything? "

She pulled open the gate and a lad of fifteen or so, his face bathed in perspiration, appeared.

He at once said:

" There's a deserter been killed . . . a German deserter."

And the three women were forthwith overcome with a great sense of peace. After the rush of events that had come upon them like a tempest, it seemed to them as though nothing could touch them now. The phantom of death vanished from their minds. A man had been shot, no doubt, but that didn't matter, because the man was not one of theirs. And the gladness that revived them was such that they could almost have laughed.

And, once again, Catherine appeared. She announced that Victor was returning. And the three women saw a man spurring his horse at the mouth of the pass, at the imminent risk of breaking his neck on the steep slope of the road. It was soon apparent, when the man reached the Étang-des-

Moines, that some one was following him with swift
strides; and Marthe uttered cries of joy at recognizing the tall figure of her husband.

She waved her handkerchief. Philippe answered
the signal.

"It's he!" she said, almost swooning. "It's he,
mamma. . . . I am sure that he'll be able to tell us
everything . . . and that M. Morestal is not far
off. . . ."

"Let us go and meet them," Suzanne suggested.

"Yes, I'll go," said Marthe, quickly. "You stay
here, Suzanne . . . stay with mamma."

She darted away, eager to be the first to welcome
Philippe and recovering enough strength to run to
the bottom of the slope:

"Philippe! Philippe!" she cried. "You are
back at last. . . ."

He lifted her off the ground and pressed her to
him:

"My darling, I hear that you have been uneasy.
. . . You need not have been. . . . I will tell you
all about it. . . ."

"Yes, you will tell us. . . . But come . . . come
quick and kiss your mother and reassure her. . . ."

She dragged him along. They climbed the staircase and, on reaching the terrace, he suddenly found
himself in the presence of Suzanne, who was waiting, convulsed with jealousy and hatred. Philippe's

emotion was so great that he did not even offer her
his hand.   Besides, at that moment, Mme. Morestal
ran up to him:

" Your father? "

" Alive."

And Suzanne, in her turn:

" Papa? "

" Alive also. . . . They have both been carried
off by the German police, near the frontier."

" What?   Prisoners? "

" Yes."

" They haven't hurt them? "

The three women all stood round him and pressed
him with questions.   He replied, laughing:

" A little calmness, first. . . . I confess I feel
rather dazed. . . . This makes two exciting nights
. . . Also, I am simply starving."

His shoes and clothes were grey with dust.   There
was blood on one of his shirt-cuffs.

" You are wounded! " cried Marthe.

" No . . . not I. . . . I'll explain to you. . . ."

Catherine brought him a cup of coffee, which he
swallowed greedily, and he began:

" It was about five o'clock in the morning when
I got up; and I certainly had no idea, when I left
my room . . ."

Marthe was stupefied.   Why did Philippe say
that he had slept there?   Did he not know that his

absence had been discovered? But then why tell that lie?

She instinctively placed herself in front of Suzanne and in front of her mother; and, as Philippe had broken off, himself embarrassed by the obvious commotion which he had caused, she asked him:

" So, last evening, you left your father and M. Jorancé? . . ."

" At the Carrefour du Grand-Chêne."

" Yes, so Suzanne told us. And you came back straight? "

" Straight."

" But you heard the shots fired? . . ."

" Shots? "

" Yes, on the frontier."

" No. I must have gone to sleep at once. . . . I was tired. . . . Otherwise, if I had heard them . . ."

He had an intuition of the danger which he was running, especially as Suzanne was trying to make signs to him. But he had prepared the opening of his story so carefully that, being unaccustomed to lying, he would have been unable to alter a single word of it without losing the little coolness that remained to him. Moreover, himself worn out and incapable of resisting the atmosphere of anxiety and nervousness that surrounded him, how could

he have perceived the trap which Marthe uncon-
sciously had laid for him? He, therefore, repeated:

"Once more, when I left my room, I had no
idea of what had happened. It was an accident
that put me in the way of it. I had reached the
Col du Diable and was walking along the frontier-
road when, half-way from the Butte-aux-Loups, I
heard moans and groans on my left. I went to
the spot where they came from and discovered,
among the bracken, a wounded man, covered in
blood. . . ."

"The deserter," said Mme. Morestal.

"Yes, a German private, Johann Baufeld," replied
Philippe.

He was now coming to the true portion of his
story, for his interview with the deserter had really
taken place when he was returning from Saint-
Élophe, at break of day; and he continued, with an
easier mind:

"Johann Baufeld had only a few minutes to live.
He had the death-rattle in his throat. Nevertheless, he had strength enough left to tell me his
name and to speak a few words; and he died in
my arms, not, however, before I learnt from him
that M. Jorancé and my father had tried to protect
him on French territory and that the police had
turned upon them. I therefore went in search of

them. The track was easy to follow. It took me through the Col du Diable to the hamlet of Torins. There, the inn-keeper made no difficulty about telling me that a squad of police, several of whom were mounted, had passed his house on their way to Börsweilen, where they were conveying two French prisoners. One of these was wounded. I could not find out if it was your father, Suzanne, or mine. In any case, the wounds must have been slight, for both prisoners were sitting their horses without assistance. I felt reassured and turned back. At the Col du Diable, I met Victor. . . . You know the rest."

He seemed quite happy at finishing his story and poured himself out a second cup of coffee, with the satisfied air of a man who has got off cheaply.

The three women were silent. Suzanne lowered her head, lest she should betray her emotion. At last, Marthe, who had no suspicions, but who was worrying her head about Philippe's falsehood, resumed:

" At what time did you come in last night? "

" At a quarter to eleven."

" And you went to bed at once? "

" At once."

" Then how is it that your bed has not been touched? "

Philippe gave a start. The question took his

breath away. Instead of inventing some pretext or other, he stammered, guilelessly:

" Oh, so you went in . . . you saw . . ."

He had not thought of this detail, nor, for that matter, of any of those which might make his story appear to clash with the facts; and he no longer knew what to say.

Suzanne suggested:

" Perhaps Philippe spent the night in a chair. . . ."

Marthe shrugged her shoulders; and Philippe, utterly at a loss, trying to make up another version, did not even answer. He remained dumb, like a child caught at fault.

" Come, Philippe," asked Marthe, " what's underneath this? Didn't you come straight back? "

" No," he admitted.

" You came back by the frontier? "

" Yes."

" Then why conceal it? I couldn't very well be anxious now, seeing that you are here."

" That's just it!" cried Philippe, plunging at a venture along this path. " That's just it! I did not want to tell you that I had spent the night looking for my father."

" The night! Then you knew before this morning that he had been carried off? "

" Yes, last evening."

"Last evening? But how? Who told you? You can only have known it by witnessing the arrest."

He hesitated for a second. He could have dated his interview with the deserter Baufeld to that particular moment. But he did not think of this; and he declared, in a firm tone:

"Well, yes, I was there . . . or, at least, not far off. . . ."

"And you heard the shots?"

"Yes, I heard the shots and also some cries of pain. . . . When I arrived on the scene of the fighting, there was no one there. Then I hunted about. . . . You understand, I was afraid that my father or M. Jorancé had been hit by the bullets. . . . I hunted all night, following their track in the dark: a wrong track, first of all, which led me towards the Albern Woods. And then, this morning, I found Private Baufeld, who told me which way the attacking party had gone, and I pushed on to the factory and to the inn at Torins. But if I had told you all that, oh, by Jove, how you would have fretted about my fatigue! Why, I can picture you doing so, my poor Marthe!"

He pretended to be gay and careless. Marthe watched him in astonishment. She nodded her head with a thoughtful air:

" Yes . . . you are right. . . ."

" Don't you think so? It was much simpler to tell you that I had just left my room, feeling fit and well, after a good night's rest. . . . Don't you agree with me, mother? . . . Besides, you your-self . . ."

But, at that moment, a sound of voices rose under the windows on the garden-side and Catherine burst into the room, yelling :

" The master! The master!"

And Victor also bounded in :

" Here's the master coming! There he is!"

" Who? Who?" asked Mme. Morestal, hasten-ing forward.

" M. Morestal! There he is! We saw him at the end of the garden. . . . Look, over there, near the water-fall. . . ."

The old lady ran to one of the windows :

" Yes! He has seen us! O God, is it possible?"

Staggering with excitement, she leant heavily on Marthe's arm and dragged her to the staircase that led to the front hall and the steps.

They had hardly disappeared when Suzanne flung herself upon Philippe :

" Oh, please, Philippe . . . please!" she im-plored.

He did not understand at first :

"What is it, Suzanne?"

"Please, please be careful. Don't let Marthe suspect. . . ."

"Do you think . . .?"

"I thought so, for a second. . . . She gave me such a queer look. . . . Oh, it would be terrible! . . . Please, please . . ."

She left him quickly, but her words and the scared look in her eyes gave Philippe a real fright. Hitherto, he had felt towards Marthe only the embarrassment provoked by the annoyance of having to tell a lie. He now suddenly perceived the full gravity of the situation, the peril which threatened Suzanne and which might shatter the happiness of his own household. One blunder . . . and everything was discovered. And this thought, instead of clearing his brain forthwith, merely increased his confusion.

"I must save Suzanne," he repeated. "Above all, I must save Suzanne."

But he felt that he had no more power over the events at hand than a man has over the approaching storm. And a dull fear arose within his breast.

CHAPTER III

FATHER AND SON

BARE-HEADED, tangle-haired, his clothes torn, no collar, blood on his shirt, on his hands, on his face, blood everywhere, a wound in his neck, another on his lip, unrecognizable, horrible to look at, but magnificent in energy, heroic and triumphant: such was the appearance presented by old Morestal.

He chortled:

"Here!" he shouted.

An enormous laugh rolled from under his moustache:

"Morestal? Here! . . . Morestal, for the second time, a prisoner of the Teuton . . . and, for the second time, free!"

Philippe stared at him in dismay, as though at an apparition.

"Well, sonny? Is that the way you welcome me home?"

He caught hold of a napkin and wiped his face with a great, wide gesture. Then he drew his wife to him:

"Kiss me, mother! . . . And you, Philippe!

And you, Marthe! . . . And you too, my pretty
Suzanne: once for myself and once for your father!
. . . Don't cry, my child. . . . Daddy's all right.
. . . They're coddling him like an emperor, over
there . . . until they let him go. And that's not
far off. By Heaven, no! I hope the French government . . ."

He was talking like a drunken man, too fast and
in an unsteady voice. His wife tried to make him
sit down. He protested:

"Rest? Quite unnecessary, mother. A Morestal
never rests. My wounds? Scratches! What?
The doctor? If he sets foot in this house, I'll chuck
him out of the window!"

"Still, you ought to take something. . . ."

"Take something? A glass of wine, if you like
. . . a glass of good French wine. . . . That's it,
uncork a bottle. . . . We'll have a glass all round.
. . . Your health, Weisslicht! . . . Oh, what a
joke! . . . When I think of the face of Weisslicht,
the special commissary of the imperial government!
. . . The prisoner's gone! The bird's flown!"

He laughed loudly and, after drinking two
glasses of wine, one on top of the other, he kissed
the three women once more, kissed Philippe, called
in Victor, Catherine, the gardener, shook hands with
them, sent them away again and began to walk up
and down the room, saying:

"No time to be lost, children! I met the sergeant of gendarmes on the Saint-Élophe road. The authorities have been informed. . . . They can be here within half an hour. I want to present a report. Take a pen, Philippe."

"What's much more important," protested his wife, "is that you should not excite yourself like this. Here, tell us all about it instead, quite calmly."

Old Morestal was never known to refuse to talk. He therefore began his story, in short, slow sentences, as she wished, describing all the details of attack and all the incidents of the journey to Börsweilen. But, carried away once more, he raised his voice, grew indignant, worked himself into a rage, burst into sarcasm:

"Oh, they showed no lack of civility! . . . It was, 'Monsieur le commissaire spécial! . . . Monsieur le conseiller d'arrondissement·!' . . . Weisslicht had his mouth crammed with our titles! . . . All the same, at one o'clock in the morning, we were safely locked up in two nice little rooms in the town-hall at Börsweilen. . . . In quod, what! . . . With a probable indictment for complicity, espionage, high treason and the devil knows what hanging over our heads! . . . Only, in that case, gentlemen, you should not carry politeness so far as to release your captives from their handcuffs; and the windows of your cells ought not to be closed with bars too slight to be of any use; and you ought not to let one of your prisoners keep his pocket-knife. If you do, as long as that prisoner has any grit in him — and a file to his knife, by Jove! — he will try what he can do. And I did try, by Jingo! At four o'clock in the morning, after cutting the window-pane and filing or loosening four of the bars, old Morestal let himself down by a waste-pipe and took to his heels. Kind friends, farewell! . . . It was now only a question of getting home. . . . The Col du Diable? The Albern Woods? The Butte-aux-Loups? No such fool! The vermin were bound to be swarming on that side. . . . And, in fact, I heard the drums beating and the trumpets sounding the alarm and the horses galloping. They were hunting for me, of course! . . . But how could they have thought of hunting for me six miles away, in the Val de Sainte-Marie, right in the middle of the Forest of Arzance? And I trotted . . . I trotted until I was simply done. . . . I crossed the border at eight o'clock, unseen and unknown. Morestal's foot was on his native heath! At ten o'clock, I saw the steeple of Saint-Élophe from the Côte-Blanche and I cut straight across, so as to get home quicker. And here I am! A bit tired, I admit, but quite presentable. . . . Well, what do you say to old Morestal now, eh?"

He had stood up and, forgetting all about the fatigue of the night, was enlivening his discourse with a savage display of gesture which alarmed his wife.

" And my poor father was not able to escape? " asked Suzanne.

" No, they had taken care to search him," replied Morestal. " Besides, they watched him more closely than they did me . . . so he could not do as I did. . . ." And he added. " And a good job too! For I should have been left to languish in their prisons until the end of an interminable trial; whereas he, in forty-eight hours . . . But this is all talk. The authorities can't be far away. I want to have my report ready. There are certain things which I suspect . . . the business was a plot from start to finish. . . ."

He interrupted himself, as though startled by an unexpected thought, and sat for a long time motionless, with his head in his hands. Then, suddenly, he struck the table with his fist:

" That's it! I understand the whole thing now! Upon my word, it's taken me long enough! "

" What? " asked his wife.

" Dourlowski, of course! "

" Dourlowski? "

" Why, yes! From the first minute, I guessed that it was a trap, a trap contrived by inferior po-

lice-agents. But how was it laid? I see it now.
Dourlowski came here yesterday, on some pretext
or other. He knew that Jorancé and I would take
the frontier-road in the evening; and the passing
of the deserter was contrived to take place at that
moment, in connivance with the German detectives!
One of them whistles as soon as we come up; and
the soldier, who has been told, of course, that this
whistle is a signal from the French accomplices, the
soldier, whom Dourlowski or his confederates hold
in a leash, like a dog, the soldier is let go. That's
the whole mystery! It was not he, the poor wretch,
whom they were after, but Jorancé and Morestal.
Morestal, right enough, flies to the rescue of the
fugitive. They collar him, they lay hold of Jorancé; and there we are, accomplices both. Bravo,
gentlemen! Well played!"

Mme. Morestal murmured:

"But, I say, it might be a serious thing . . ."

"For Jorancé," he replied, "yes, because he is in
custody; only — there is an 'only'— the pursuit
of the deserter took place on French soil. We also
were arrested on French soil. It was a flagrant
violation of the frontier. So there's nothing to
be afraid of."

"You think so?" asked Suzanne. "You think
that my father . . . ?"

"Nothing to be afraid of," repeated Morestal.

And he declared, positively, " I look upon Jorancé
as free."

" Tut, tut! " mumbled the old lady. " Things
won't go so fast as that."

" Once more, I look upon Jorancé as free and
for this good reason, that the frontier has been vio-
lated."

" Who will prove the violation? "

" Who? Why, I, of course! . . . And Jorancé!
. . . Do you think they'll doubt the word of honest
men like us? Besides, there are other proofs.
They will find the traces of the pursuit, the traces
of the attack, the traces of the stand which we made.
And who can tell? There may have been witnesses. . . ."

Marthe turned her eyes on Philippe. He was
listening to his father, with a face so pale that she
was astounded. She waited for a few seconds and
then, seeing that he did not speak, she said:

" There was a witness."

Morestal started:

" What's that, Marthe? "

" Philippe was there."

" Nonsense! We left Philippe at the Carrefour
du Grand-Chêne, at the bottom of the hill, didn't
we, Suzanne? You remained behind together."

Philippe intervened, quickly:

" Suzanne went off at once! and so did I . . .

but I had not gone two hundred yards when I turned back."

" So that was why you did not answer when I called to you, half-way up the hill? "

" I expect so.   I went back to the Grand-Chêne."

" What for? "

" To join you. . . . I was sorry I had left you."

" Then you were behind us at the time of the attack? "

" Yes."

" In that case, of course, you heard the shots fired! . . . Let me see, you must have been on the Butte-aux-Loups. . . ."

" Somewhere near there. . . ."

" And perhaps you saw us. . . . From above! . . . With the moonlight! . . ."

" Oh, no! " protested Philippe.   " No, I saw nothing! "

" But, if you heard the firing, you must certainly have heard Jorancé shouting. . . . They stuffed a gag into my mouth. . . . But Jorancé kept on roaring, ' We are in France! We are on French territory!' You heard Jorancé shouting, didn't you, now? "

Philippe hesitated before making a reply of which he vaguely felt the tremendous importance. But, opposite him, he saw Marthe watching him with increasing surprise and, near Marthe, he saw Suzanne's drawn features. He said:

"Yes, I heard him . . . I heard him at a distance. . . ."

Old Morestal could not contain himself for joy. And, when he learnt besides that Philippe had received the last words of Baufeld the deserter, he burst out:

"You saw him? He was alive? He told you that they had set a trap for us, didn't he?"

"He mentioned the name of Dourlowski."

"Capital! But our meeting with the soldier, the pursuit . . . he must have told you that all this took place in France?"

"Yes, I seemed to understand . . ."

"We've got them!" shouted Morestal. "We've got them! Of course, I was quite easy in my mind. . . . But all the same, Philippe's evidence, the declaration of the dying private. . . . Ah, the brigands, they'll have to let go their prey! . . . We were in France, kind friends! There has been a violation of the frontier!"

Philippe saw that he had gone too far; and he objected:

"My evidence is not evidence in the proper sense of the word. . . . As for the soldier, I could hardly make out . . ."

" We've got them, I tell you. The little that you were able to see, the little that you were able to hear all agrees with my own evidence, that is to say, with the truth. We've got them! And here come the gentlemen from the public prosecutor's office, who will be of my opinion, I bet you what you like! And it won't take long either! Jorancé will be free to-morrow."

He dropped the pen, which he had taken up in order to write his report himself, and went quickly to the window, attracted by the sound of a motor-car sweeping round the garden-lawn:

" The sub-prefect," he said. " By Jove, so the government know about it! The examining-magistrate and the prosecutor. . . . Ha, ha, they are not wasting any time, I see! . . . Quick, mother, have them shown in here. . . . I'll be back in a minute: I must just put on a collar and change my jacket. . . ."

" Father! "

Morestal stopped in the doorway:

" What is it, my boy? " he asked.

" I have something to say to you," said Philippe, resolutely.

" All right. But it'll keep until presently, won't it?"

" I have something to say to you now."

" Oh! In that case, come along with me. Yes,

you can give me a hand, instead of Victor, who is out."

And, laughing, he went to his room.

Marthe involuntarily took a few steps, as though she proposed to be present at the conversation. Philippe experienced a momentary embarrassment. Then he quickly made up his mind:

"No, Marthe, you had better stay."

"But . . ."

"No, once more, no. Excuse me. I will explain later. . . ."

And he followed his father.

As soon as they were alone, Morestal, who was thinking much more about his evidence than about Philippe's words, asked, casually:

"Is it private?"

"Yes . . . and very serious," Philippe declared.

"Nonsense!"

"Very serious, as you will see in a moment, father. . . . It's about a position in which I find myself placed, a horrible position which I don't know how to get out of, unless . . ."

He went no further. Acting under an instinctive impulse, thrown off his balance by the arrival of the examining-magistrate and by a sudden vision of the events to come, he had appealed to his father.

He wanted to speak, to say the words that would deliver him. What words? He did not quite know. But anything, anything rather than give false evidence and affix his signature to a lying deposition!

He stammered at first, while his brain refused to act, seeking in vain for an acceptable solution. How was he to stop on the downward course along which he was being dragged by a combination of hostile forces, accidents, coincidences and implacable, trifling facts? How was he to break through the circle which a cruel fate was doing its utmost to trace around him?

It suddenly burst in upon him that the only possible way out lay in proclaiming the immediate truth, in bluntly revealing his conduct.

He shuddered with disgust. What! Accuse Suzanne! Was that the half-formed idea that inspired him, unknown to himself? Had he really thought of ruining her in order that he might be saved? It was now that he first realized the full nature of his predicament, for he would a thousand times rather have died than dishonour the girl, even in his father's eyes alone.

Morestal, who had finished dressing, chaffed him:

"Is that all you wanted to say?"

"Yes. . . . I made a mistake," replied Philippe. "I thought . . ."

He was leaning on the window-rail and looked out inertly at the large sort of park formed by the clustering trees and the undulating meadows of the Vosges. He was now obsessed by other thoughts, which mingled with his own anxiety. He went back to old Morestal:

"Are you quite sure that the arrest took place on French soil?"

"Upon my word, you must be mad!"

"It's possible that, without noticing it, you crossed the frontier-line. . . ."

"Yes . . . exactly . . . so we did. But, at the moment of the first attack and again at the moment of the arrest, we were in France. There is no doubt about that."

"Just think, father, if there were the slightest doubt! . . ."

"Well, what then? What do you mean?"

"I mean that this incident will have further consequences. The affair will create a noise."

"What do I care? The truth comes first, surely? Once we are in the right, we are bound to see that our rights are recognized and that Jorancé is released."

Morestal planted himself firmly in front of his son:

"You're of my way of thinking, I suppose?"

"No."

"How do you mean, no?"

"Listen, father: the circumstances seem to me to be very serious. The examining-magistrate's enquiry is most important. It will serve as a basis for later enquiries. It seems to me that we ought to reflect and give our evidence with a certain reserve, with caution. . . . We must behave prudently. . . ."

"We must behave like Frenchmen who are in the right," cried Morestal, "and who, when they are in the right, fear nobody and nothing in this world!"

"Not even war?"

"War! What are you talking about? War! But there can't be war over an incident like this! The way things are shaping, Germany will yield."

"Do you think so?" said Philippe, who seemed relieved by this assertion.

"Certainly! But on one condition, that we establish our right firmly. There has been a violation of the frontier. That is beyond dispute. Let us prove it; and every chance of a conflict is removed."

"But, if we don't succeed in proving it?" asked Philippe.

"Ah, in that case, it can't be helped! . . . Of course, they will dispute it. But have no fear, my boy: the proofs exist; and we can safely go ahead.

. . . Come along, they're waiting for us downstairs. . . ."

He grasped the door-handle.

" Father ! "

" Look here, what's the matter with you to-day?
Aren't you coming? "

" No, not yet," said Philippe, who saw a way out
and who was making a last effort to escape. " Presently. . . . I must absolutely tell you. . . . You
and I start from a different point of view. . . . I
have rather different ideas from yours . . . and,
as the occasion happens to present itself . . ."

" Impossible, my boy! They are waiting for
us. . . ."

" You must hear me," cried Philippe, blocking the
way. " I refuse to accept with a light heart a responsibility that is not in accordance with my present
opinions; and that is why an explanation between
us has become inevitable."

Morestal looked at him with an air of amazement:

" Your present opinions! Ideas different from
mine! What's all this nonsense? "

Philippe felt, even more clearly than on the day
before, the violence of a conflict which a confession would provoke. But, this time, his resolve
was taken. There were too many reasons urging
him towards a breach which he considered neces-

sary. With his mind and his whole frame palpitating with his tense will, he was about to utter the irrevocable words, when Marthe hurried into the room:

"Don't keep your father, Philippe; the examining-magistrate is asking for him."

"Ah!" said Morestal. "I am not sorry that you have come to release me, my dear Marthe. Your husband's crazy. He's been talking a string of nonsense these past ten minutes. What you want, my boy, is rest."

Philippe made a slight movement. Marthe whispered:

"Be quiet."

And she said it in so imperious a tone that he was taken aback.

Before leaving the room, Morestal walked to the window. Bugle-notes sounded in the distance and he leant out to hear them better.

Marthe at once said to Philippe:

"I came in on chance. I felt that you were seeking an explanation with your father."

"Yes, I had to."

"About your ideas, I suppose?"

"Yes, I must."

"Your father is ill. . . . It's his heart. . . . A fit of anger might prove fatal . . . especially after last night. Not a word, Philippe."

At that moment, Morestal closed the window.

He passed in front of them and then, turning and placing his hand on his son's shoulder, he murmured, in accents of restrained ardour:

"Do you hear the enemy's bugle, over there? Ah, Philippe, I don't want it to become a war-song! . . . But, all the same, if it should . . . if it should! . . ."

At one o'clock on the afternoon of Tuesday the 2nd of September, Philippe, sitting opposite his father, before the pensive eyes of Marthe, before the anxious eyes of Suzanne, Philippe, after relating most minutely his conversation with the dying soldier, declared that he had heard at a distance the cries of protest uttered by Jorancé, the special commissary.

Having made the declaration, he signed it.

CHAPTER IV

THE tragedy enacted that night and morning was so harsh, so virulent and so swift that it left the inmates of the Old Mill as though stunned. Instead of uniting them in a common emotion, it scattered them, giving each of them an impression of discomfort and uneasiness.

In Philippe, this took the form of a state of torpor that kept him asleep until the next morning. He awoke, however, in excellent condition, but with an immense longing for solitude. In reality, he shrank from finding himself in the presence of his father and his wife.

He went out, therefore, very early, across the woods and fields, stopped at an inn, climbed the Ballon de Vergix and did not come home until lunch-time. He was very calm by then and quite master of himself.

To men like Philippe, men endowed with upright natures and generous minds, but not prone to waste time in reflecting upon the minor cases of conscience that arise in daily life, the sense of duty performed becomes, at critical periods, a sort of standard by which they judge their actions. This sense Philippe experienced in all its fulness. Placed by a series of abnormal circumstances between the necessity of betraying Suzanne or the necessity of swearing upon oath to a thing which he did not know, he felt that he was certainly entitled to lie. The lie seemed just and natural. He did not deny the fault which he had committed in succumbing to the young girl's fascinations and wiles: but, having committed the fault, he owed it to Suzanne to keep it secret, whatever the consequences of his discretion might be. There was no excuse that permitted him to break silence.

He found, on the drawing-room table, the three newspapers which were taken at the Old Mill: the *Eclaireur des Vosges;* a Paris evening-paper; and the *Börsweilener Zeitung,* a morning-paper printed in German, but French in tone and inspiration. A glance at these completely reassured him. Amid the confusion of the first reports devoted to the Jorancé case, his own part passed almost unnoticed. The *Éclaireur des Vosges* summoned up his evidence in a couple of lines. When all was said, he was and would be no more than a supernumerary.

"A walking gentleman, at the outside," he murmured, with satisfaction.

"Yes, at the outside.   It's your father and M. Jorancé who play the star parts."

Marthe had entered and caught his last words, which he had spoken aloud, and was answering him with a laugh.

She put her arm around his neck with the fond gesture usual to her and said:

"Yes, Philippe, you need not worry yourself. Your evidence is of no importance and cannot influence events in any way.   You can be very sure of that."

Their faces were quite close together and Philippe read nothing but gaiety and affection in Marthe's eyes.

He understood that she had ascribed his behaviour of the previous day, his first, false version, his reticence and his confusion to scruples of conscience and vague apprehensions.   Anxious about the consequences of the business and dreading lest his testimony might complicate it, he had tried to avoid the annoyance of giving evidence.

"I believe you're right," he said, with a view to confirming her in her mistake.   "Besides, is the business so very serious?"

They talked together for a few minutes and, gradually, while watching her, he changed the subject to the Jorancés:

"Has Suzanne been this morning?"

Marthe appeared astonished:

"Suzanne?" she said. "Don't you know? . . . Oh, of course, you were asleep last evening. Suzanne spent the night here."

He turned aside his head, to hide the flush that spread over his features, and he said:

"Oh, she slept here, did she?"

"Yes. M. Morestal wishes her to stay with us until M. Jorancé's return."

"But . . . but where is she now? . . ."

"She is at Börsweilen . . . she has gone to ask for leave to see her father."

"Alone?"

"No, Victor went with her."

With an air of indifference, Philippe asked:

"How is she? Depressed?"

"Very much depressed. . . . I don't know why, but she imagines that it was her fault that her father was kidnapped. . . . She says she urged him to go for that walk! . . . Poor Suzanne, what interest could she have in remaining alone? . . ."

He plainly perceived, from his wife's voice and attitude, that, although certain coincidences had surprised her, her mind had not been touched by the shadow of a suspicion. On that side, everything was over. The danger was averted.

Happily released from his fears, Philippe had the further satisfaction of learning that his father had

spent a very good night and that he had gone to
the town-hall at Saint-Élophe. He questioned his
mother. Mme. Morestal, yielding like Philippe to
that desire for assuagement and security which
comes over us after any great shock, reassured him
on the subject of the old man's health. Certainly,
there was something the matter with the heart:
Dr. Borel insisted upon his leading the most regular
and monotonous life. But Dr. Borel always looked
at the dark side of things; and, all considered,
Morestal had borne the fatigue attendant on his
capture and escape, hard though it was, very well
indeed.

"Besides, you have only to look at him," she
concluded. "Here he comes, back from Saint-
Élophe."

They saw him alight from the carriage with the
brisk and springy step of a young man. He joined
them in the drawing-room and at once cried:

"Oh, what an uproar! I've telephoned to town.
. . . They're talking of nothing else. . . . And
who do you think swooped down upon me at Saint-
Élophe? Quite half-a-dozen reporters! I sent
them away with a flea in their ears! A set of fellows who make mischief wherever they go and who
arrange everything as it suits them! . . . They're
the scourge of our time! . . . I shall give Catherine formal orders that no one is to be admitted

to the Old Mill. . . . Why, did you see how they report my escape? I'm supposed to have strangled the sentry and to have made a couple of Uhlans who pursued me bite the dust! . . ."

He could not succeed in concealing his satisfaction and drew himself to his full height, like a man who sees nothing astonishing in an exploit of that kind.

Philippe asked.

" And what is the general feeling? "

" Just what the papers say. Jorancé's release is imminent. I told you as much. The more we assert ourselves, as we have every right to do, the sooner the thing will be over. You must understand that friend Jorancé is being examined at this moment and that he is giving exactly the same replies that I did. So you see! . . . No, once more, Germany will give way. It is only a question of a day or two. So don't upset yourself, my boy, since you're so afraid of war . . . and the responsibilities attaching to it! . . ."

This, when all was said and done, was the motive to which he, like Marthe, ascribed the incoherent words which Philippe had uttered previous to his appearance before the magistrates; and, without going deeper into the matter, it gave him, on his side, a certain sense of anger, mingled with a mild contempt. Philippe Morestal, old Morestal's son, afraid of war! He was one more corrupted by the Paris poison! . . .

Lunch was very lively. The old man never ceased talking. His good-humour, his optimism, his steady belief in a favourable and immediate solution overcame every resistance; and Philippe himself was glad to share a conviction that delighted him.

The afternoon was continued under equally propitious auspices. Morestal and Philippe were sent for to the frontier, where, in the presence of the public prosecutor, the sub-prefect, the sergeant of gendarmes and a number of journalists whom they tried in vain to send away, the examining-magistrate carefully completed the investigations which he had begun the day before. Morestal had to repeat the story of the aggression on the spot where it occurred, to point definitely to the road followed before the attack and during the flight, to fix the place where Private Baufeld had crossed the frontier-line and the place where the commissary and himself were arrested.

He did so without hesitation, walking to and fro, talking and making his statements so positively, so logically and so sincerely that the scene, as pictured by him, lived again before the spectators' eyes. His demonstration was lucid and commanding. Here, the first shot was fired. There, a sharp divergence to the right, on German territory. Here, back in France and, further on, at that exact spot, fifteen yards on this side of the frontier, the scene of the fight, the place of the arrest. Indications, undeniable indications, abounded. It was the truth, with no possible fear of a mistake.

Philippe was carried away and categorically confirmed his original declaration. He had heard the special commissary shouting, as he approached the Butte-aux-Loups. The words, " We are in France! . . . There is the frontier!" had reached him distinctly. And he described his search, his conversation with Private Baufeld and the wounded man's evidence concerning the encroachment on French territory.

The enquiry ended with a piece of good news. On Monday, a few hours before the attack, Farmer Saboureux was said to have seen Weisslicht, the chief of the German detectives, and a certain Dourlowski, a hawker, walking in the woods and trying to keep hidden. Now Morestal, without confessing the relations that existed between him and that individual, had nevertheless spoken of the visit of this Dourlowski and of his proposal that the witness should act as an accomplice. An understanding between Dourlowski and Weisslicht was a proof that an ambush had been laid and that the passing of Private Baufeld across the frontier, arranged for half-past ten, was only a pretext to catch the special commissary and his friend in a trap.

The magistrates made no secret of their satisfaction. The Jorancé case, a plot hatched by subordinate officials of police, whom the imperial government would not hesitate to disown was becoming rapidly reduced to the proportions of an incident which would lead to nothing and be forgotten on the morrow.

" That's all right," said Morestal, walking away with his son, while the magistrates went on to Saboureux's Farm. " It will be an even simpler matter than I hoped. The French government will know the results of the enquiry this evening. There will be an exchange of views with the German embassy; and to-morrow . . ."

" Do you think so? . . ."

" I go further. I believe that Germany will make the first advance."

As they came to the Col du Diable, they passed a small company of men headed by one in a gold-laced cap.

Morestal took off his hat with a flourish and grinned:

" Good-afternoon! . . . I hope I see you well!"

The man passed without speaking.

" Who is that? " asked Philippe.

" Weisslicht, the chief of the detectives."

" And the others? "

" The others? . . . It's the Germans making their investigation."

It was then four o'clock in the afternoon.

The remainder of that day passed peacefully at the Old Mill. Suzanne arrived from Börsweilen at nightfall, looking radiant. They had given her a letter from her father and she would be authorized to see him on Saturday.

" You will not even have to go back to Börsweilen," said Morestal. " Your father will come to fetch you here, won't he, Philippe? "

Dinner brought them all five together under the family lamp; and they experienced a feeling of relaxation, comfort and repose. They drank to the special commissary's health. And it seemed to them as if his place were not even empty, so great was the certainty with which they expected his return.

Philippe was the only one who did not share in the general gaiety. Sitting beside Marthe and opposite Suzanne, he was bound, with his upright nature and his sane judgment, to suffer at finding himself situated in such a false position. Since the night before last, since the moment when he had left Suzanne while the dawning light of day stole into her room at Saint-Élophe, this was the first instant that he had had any sort of time to conjure up the memory of those unnerving hours. Alarmed by the course of events, obsessed by his anxiety about the way in which he was to act, his one and only thought of Suzanne had been how not to compromise her.

Now, he saw her before him. He heard her laugh and talk. She lived in his presence, not as he had known her in Paris and found her at Saint-Élophe, but adorned with a different charm, of which he knew the mysterious secret. True, he remained master of himself and he clearly felt that no temptation would induce him to succumb a second time. But could he help it that she had fair hair, the colour of which bewitched him, and quivering lips and a voice melodious as a song? And could he help it that all this filled him with an emotion which every minute that passed made more profound?

Their eyes met. Suzanne trembled under Philippe's gaze. A sort of bashfulness decked her as with a veil that gives added beauty to its wearer. She was as desirable as a wife and as winsome as a bride.

At that moment, Marthe smiled to Philippe. He turned red and thought:

" I shall go away to-morrow."

His decision was taken then and there. He would not remain a day longer between the two women. The mere sight of their intimacy was hateful to him. He would go away without a word. He knew the danger of leave-takings between people who love, knew how they soften us and disarm us. He wanted none of those compromises and evasions. Temptation, even if we resist it, is a fault in itself.

When dinner was over, he stood up and went to his bedroom, where Marthe joined him. He learnt from her that Suzanne's room was on the same floor. Later, he heard the young girl come upstairs. But he knew that nothing would make him fall again.

As soon as he was alone, he opened his window, sat a long time staring at the vague outlines of the trees, then undressed and went to bed.

In the morning, Marthe brought him his letters. He at once recognized the writing of a friend on one of the envelopes:

" Good! " he said, jumping at the pretext. " A

letter from Pierre Belum. I hope it's not to tell
me to come back!"

He opened the letter and, after reading it, said:
" It's as I feared! I shall have to go."

" Not before this evening, my boy."

It was old Morestal, who had entered the room
with an open letter in his hand.

" What's the matter, father?"

" We are specially summoned to appear before
the Prefect of the Vosges in the town-hall at Saint-
Élophe."

" I too?"

" You too. They want to verify certain points in
your deposition."

" So they are beginning all over again?"

" Yes, it's a fresh enquiry. It appears that
things are becoming complicated."

" What are you saying?"

" I am saying what this morning's papers say.
According to the latest telegrams, Germany has no
intention of releasing Jorancé. Moreover, there
have been manifestations in Paris. Berlin also is
stirring. The yellow press are adopting an arro-
gant tone. In short . . ."

" What?"

" Well, the matter is taking a very nasty turn."

Philippe gave a start. He walked up to his father and, yielding to a sudden fit of anger:

"There! Which of us was right? You see, you see what's happening now! If you had listened to me . . ."

"If I had listened to you? . . ." echoed Morestal, emphasizing each word and at once preparing for a quarrel.

But Philippe restrained himself. Marthe made a remark or two at random. And then all three were silent.

Besides, of what use was speech? The thunderstorm had passed over their heads and was rumbling over France. Henceforward powerless, they must undergo its consequences and hear its distant echoes without being able to influence the formidable elements that had been let loose during that Monday night.

CHAPTER V

THE German argument was simple enough: the arrest had taken place in Germany. At least, that
was what the newspapers stated in the extracts
which Philippe and his father read in the *Börsweilener Zeitung*. Was it not to be expected that
this would be the argument eventually adopted —
if it was not adopted already — by the imperial
government?

At Börsweilen — the *Zeitung* made no mystery
about it — people were very positive. After
twenty-four hours' silence, the authorities took their
stand upon the explanation given the day before
by Weisslicht, in the course of an enquiry attended
by several functionaries, who were mentioned by
name; and they declared aloud that everything had
taken place in due form and that it was impossible
to go back upon accomplished facts. Special Commissary Jorancé and Councillor Morestal, caught
in the act of assisting a deserter, would be brought
before the German courts and their case tried in

accordance with German law. Besides, it was added, there were other charges against them.

Of Dourlowski, there was no mention. He was ignored.

"But the whole case depends upon him!" exclaimed Morestal, after receiving the Prefect of the Vosges at the Saint-Élophe town-hall and discussing the German argument with him and the examining-magistrate. "The whole case depends upon him, monsieur le préfet. Even supposing their argument to be correct, what is it worth, if we prove that we were drawn into an ambush by Weisslicht and that Baufeld's desertion was a got-up job contrived by subordinate officials of police? And the proof of this rests upon Dourlowski!"

He was indignant at the hawker's disappearance. But he added:

"Fortunately, we have Farmer Saboureux's evidence."

"We had it yesterday," said the examining-magistrate, "but we haven't it to-day."

"How so?"

"Yesterday, Wednesday, when I was questioning him, Farmer Saboureux declared that he had seen Weisslicht and Dourlowski together. He even used certain words which made me suspect that he had noticed the preparations for the attack and that he was an unseen witness of it . . . and a valuable witness, as you will agree. This morning, Thursday, he retracts, he is not sure that it was Weisslicht he saw and, at night, he was asleep . . . he heard nothing . . . not even the shooting. . . . And he lives at five hundred yards from the spot!"

"I never heard of such a thing! What does he mean by backing out like that?"

"I can't say," replied the magistrate. "Still, I saw a copy of the *Börsweilener Zeitung* sticking out of his pocket . . . things have altered since yesterday . . . and Saboureux has been reflecting. . . ."

"Do you think so? Is he afraid of war?"

"Yes, afraid of reprisals. He told me an old story about Uhlans, about a farm that was burnt down. So that's what it is: he's afraid! . . ."

* * *

The day began badly. Morestal and his son walked silently by the old road to the frontier, where the enquiry was resumed in detail. But, at the Butte, they saw three men in gold-laced caps smoking their pipes by the German frontier-post.

And, further on, at the foot of the slope, in a sort of clearing on the left, they perceived two more, lying flat on their stomachs, who were also smoking.

And, around these two, there were a number of freshly-painted black-and-yellow stakes, driven into the ground in a circle and roped together.

In reply to a question put to them, the men said that that was the place where Commissary Jorancé had been arrested.

Now this place, adopted by the hostile enquiry, was on German territory and at twenty yards beyond the road that marked the dividing-line between the two countries!

Philippe had to drag his father away. Old Morestal was choking with rage:

" They are lying! They are lying! It's scandalous . . . And they know it! Is it likely I should be mistaken? Why, I belong here! Whereas they . . . a pack of police-spies! . . ."

When he had grown calmer, he began his explanations over again. Philippe next repeated his, in less definite terms, this time, and with a hesitation which old Morestal, absorbed in his grievances, did not observe, but which could not well escape the others.

The father and son returned to the Old Mill together, as on the day before. Morestal was no longer so triumphant and Philippe thought of Farmer Saboureux, who, warned by his peasant shrewdness, varied his evidence according to the threat of possible events.

As soon as he reached home, he took refuge in his room. Marthe went up to him and found him lying on the bed, with his head between his hands. He would not even answer when she spoke to him. But, at four o'clock, hearing that his father, eager for news, had ordered the carriage, he went downstairs.

They drove to Saint-Élophe and then, growing more and more anxious, to Noirmont, twelve miles beyond it, where Morestal had many friends. One of these took them to the offices of the *Éclaireur*.

Here, nothing was known as yet: the telegraph- and telephone-wires were blocked. But, at eight o'clock, a first telegram got through: groups of people had raised manifestations outside the German embassy. On the Place de la Concorde, the statue of the city of Strasburg was covered with flags and flowers.

Then the telegrams flowed in.

Questioned in the Chamber, the prime minister had replied, amid the applause of the whole house:

" We ask, we claim your absolute confidence, your blind confidence. If some of you refuse it to the minister, at least grant it to the Frenchman. For it is a Frenchman who speaks in your name. And it is a Frenchman who will act."

In the lobby outside the house, a member of the opposition had begun to sing the *Marseillaise,* which was taken up by all the rest of the members in chorus.

And then there was the other side of the question: telegrams from Germany; the yellow press rabid; all the evening-papers adopting an uncompromising, aggressive attitude; Berlin in uproar. . . .

They drove back at midnight; and, although they were both seized with a like emotion, it aroused in them ideas so different that they did not exchange a word. Morestal himself, who was not aware of the divorce that had taken place between their minds, dared not indulge in his usual speeches.

The next morning, the *Börsweilener Zeitung* announced movements of troops towards the frontier. The emperor, who was cruising in the North Sea, had landed at Ostende. The chancellor was waiting for him at Cologne. And it was thought that the French ambassador had also gone to meet him.

Thenceforward, throughout that Friday and the following Saturday, the inmates of the Old Mill lived in a horrible nightmare. The storm was now shaking the whole of France and Germany, the whole of quivering Europe. They heard it roar. The earth cracked under its fury. What terrible catastrophe would it produce?

And they, who had let it loose — the actors of no account, relegated to the background, the supernumeraries whose parts were played — they could see nothing of the spectacle but distant, blood-red gleams.

Philippe took refuge in a fierce silence that distressed his wife. Morestal was nervous, excited and in an execrable temper. He went out for no reason, came in again at once, could not keep still:

" Ah," he cried, in a moment of despondency in which his thoughts stood plainly revealed, " why did we come home by the frontier? Why did I help that deserter? For there's no denying it: if I hadn't helped him, nothing would have happened."

On Friday evening, it became known that the chancellor, who already had the German reports in his hands, now possessed the French papers, which had been communicated by our ambassador. The affair, hitherto purely administrative, was becoming diplomatic. And the government was demanding the release of the special commissary of Saint-Élophe, who had been arrested on French territory.

" If they consent, all will be well," said Morestal. " There is no humiliation for Germany in disowning the action of a pack of minor officials. But, if they refuse, if they believe the policemen's lies, what will happen then? France cannot give way."

On Saturday morning, the *Börsweilener Zeitung* printed the following short paragraph in a special edition:

"After making a careful examination of the French papers, the chancellor has returned them to the French ambassador. The case of Commissary Jorancé, accused of the crime of high treason and arrested on German territory, will be tried in the German courts."

It was a refusal.

That morning, Morestal took his son to the Col du Diable and, bent in two, following the road to the Butte-aux-Loups step by step, examining each winding turn, noting a big root here and a long branch there, he reconstituted the plan of the attack. And he showed Philippe the trees against which he had brushed in his flight and the trees at the foot of which he and his friend had stood and defended themselves:

"It was there, Philippe, and nowhere else. . . . Do you see that little open space? That's where it was. . . . I have often come and smoked my pipe here, because of this little mound to sit upon. . . . That's the place!"

He sat down on the same mound and said no more, staring before him, while Philippe looked at him. Several times, he repeated, between his teeth:

" Yes, this is certainly the place. . . . How could I be mistaken?"

And, suddenly, he pressed his two fists to his temples and blurted out:

" Still, suppose I were mistaken! Suppose I had branched off more to the right . . . and . . ."

He interrupted himself, cast his eyes around him, rising to his feet:

" It's impossible! One can't make as big a blunder as that, short of being mad! How could I have? I was thinking of one thing only; I kept saying to myself, ' I must remain in France, I must keep to the left of the line.' And I did keep to it, hang it all! It is absolutely certain. . . . What then? Am I to deny the truth in order to please them?"

And Philippe, who had never ceased watching him, replied, within himself:

" Why not, father? What would that little falsehood signify, compared with the magnificent result that would be obtained? If you would tell a lie, father, or if only you would assert so fatal a truth less forcibly, France could give way without the least disgrace, since it is your evidence alone that compels her to make her demand! And, in this way, you would have saved your country. . . ."

But he did not speak. His father was guided
by a conception of duty which Philippe knew to be
as lofty and as legitimate as his own. What right
had he to expect his father to act according to his,
Philippe's, conscience? What to one of them would
be only a fib would be to the other, to old Morestal,
a criminal betrayal of his own side. Morestal,
when giving his evidence, was speaking in the name
of France. And France does not tell lies.

" If there is a possible solution," Philippe said to
himself, " my father is not the man to be asked to
provide it. My father represents a mass of in-
tangible ideas, principles and traditions. But I, I,
I . . . what can I do? What is my particular
duty? What is the object for which I ought to
make in spite of every obstacle? "

Twenty times over, he was on the point of exclaiming:

" My evidence was false, father. I was not
there. I was with Suzanne! "

What was the use? It meant dishonouring Suzanne; and the implacable march of events would
continue just the same. Now that was the only
thing that mattered. Every individual suffering,
every attack of conscience, every theory, all vanished before the tremendous catastrophe with which
humanity was threatened and before the task that
devolved upon men like himself, men emancipated

from the past and free to act in accordance with a new conception of duty.

In the afternoon, they heard at the offices of the *Éclaireur* that a bomb had burst behind the German ambassador's motor-car in Paris. In the Latin Quarter, the ferment was at its height. Two Germans had been roughly handled and a Russian, accused of spying, had been knocked down. There had been free fights at Lyons, Toulouse and Bordeaux.

Similar disorders had taken place in Berlin and in the other big towns of the German Empire. The military party was directing the movement.

Lastly, at six o'clock, it was announced as certain that Germany was mobilizing three army-corps.

A tragic evening was spent at the Old Mill. Suzanne arrived from Börsweilen without having been allowed to see her father and added to the general distress by her sobs and lamentations. Morestal and Philippe, silent and fever-eyed, seemed to avoid each other. Marthe, who suspected her husband's anguish, kept her eyes fixed upon him, as though she feared some inconsiderate act on his part. And the same dread seemed to trouble Mme. Morestal, for she warned Philippe, time after time:

" Whatever you do, no arguments with your fa-

ther.   He is not well.   All this business upsets him
quite enough as it is.   A quarrel between the two
of you would be terrible."

And this also, the idea of this illness of which
he did not know the exact nature, but to which his
heated imagination lent an added importance, this
also tortured Philippe.

They all rose on the Sunday morning with the
certainty that the news of war would reach them
in the course of the day; and old Morestal was on
the point of leaving for Saint-Élophe, to make the
necessary arrangements in case of an alarm, when
a ring of the telephone stopped him.   It was the
sub-prefect at Noirmont, who conveyed a fresh
order to him from the prefecture.   The two Morestals were to be at the Butte-aux-Loups at twelve
o'clock.

A moment later, a telegram that appeared at the
top of the front page of the *Éclaireur des Vosges*
told them the meaning of this third summons:

" The German ambassador called on the prime
minister at ten o'clock yesterday, Saturday, evening.   After a long conversation, when on the point
of concluding an interview that seemed unable to
lead to any result, the ambassador received by ex-

press a personal note from the emperor, which he
at once handed to the prime minister. In this
note, the emperor proposed a renewed examination
of the affair, for which purpose he would delegate
the Governor of Alsace-Lorraine, with instructions
to check the report of the police. An understanding was at once arrived at on this basis; and the
French government has appointed a member of the
cabinet, M. Le Corbier, under-secretary of state for
home affairs, to act as its representative. It is possible that an interview may take place between these
two prominent personages."

And the newspaper added:

" This intervention on the part of the emperor
is a proof of his peaceful intentions, but it can
hardly be said to alter the situation. If France
be in the wrong — and it were almost to be hoped
that she may be — then France will yield. But, if
it be once more proved on our side that the arrest
took place on French soil and if Germany refuse
to yield, what will happen then? "

CHAPTER VI

THE BUTTE-AUX-LOUPS

WHATEVER might be the eventual outcome of this last effort, it was a respite granted to the two nations. It gave a gleam of hope, it left a loop-hole, a chance of an arrangement.

And old Morestal, seized with fresh confidence and already triumphant, rejoiced, as he could not fail to do:

"Why, of course," he concluded, "it will all be settled! Didn't I tell you so from the beginning, Philippe? It only wanted a little firmness. . . . We have spoken clearly; and, at once, under a show of conciliation which will deceive no one, the enemy forms a plan of retreat. For, mark you, that's all that it means. . . ."

And, as he continued to read the paper, he exclaimed:

"Ah, just so! . . . I understand! . . . Listen, Philippe, to this little telegram, which sounds like nothing at all: 'England has recalled her squadrons from foreign waters and is concentrating them in the Channel and in the North Sea.' Aha, that

solves the mystery! They have reflected . . . and
reflection is the mother of wisdom. . . . And here,
Philippe, this other telegram, which is worth noting: 'Three hundred French aviators, from every
part of France, have responded to the rousing appeal issued by Captain Lériot of the territorials,
the hero of the Channel crossing. They will all
be at Châlons camp on Tuesday, with their aero-
planes!' . . . Ha, what do you say to that, my
boy? On the one side, the British fleet. . . . On
the other side, our air fleet. . . . Wipe your pretty
eyes, my sweet Suzanne, and get supper ready this
evening for Papa Jorancé! Ah, this time, mother,
we'll drink champagne!"

His gaiety sounded a little forced and found no
echo in his hearers. Philippe remained silent, with
his forehead streaked with a wrinkle which Marthe
knew well. From his appearance, from the tired
look of his eyelids, she felt certain that he had
sat up all night, examining the position from every
point of view and seeking the best road to follow.
Had he taken a resolution? And, if so, which?
He seemed so hard, so stern, so close and reticent
that she dared not ask him.

After a hastily-served meal, Morestal, on the re-
ceipt of a second telephonic communication, hurried
off to Saint-Élophe, where M. Le Corbier, the under-secretary of state, was waiting for him.

Philippe, the time of whose summons had been postponed, went to his room and locked himself in.

When he came down again, he found Marthe and Suzanne, who had decided to go with him. Mme. Morestal took him aside and, for the last time, urged him to look after his father.

The three of them walked away to the Col du Diable. A lowering sky, heavy with clouds, hung over the mountain-tops; but the weather was mild and the swards, studded with trees, still wore a look of summer.

Marthe, to break the silence, said:

" There is something soft and peaceful about the air to-day. That's a good sign. It will influence the people who are conducting the enquiry. For everything depends upon their humour, their impression, the state of their nerves, does it not, Philippe? "

" Yes," he said, " everything depends on them."

She continued:

" I don't think that they will ask you any questions. Your evidence is of such little importance. You see, the papers hardly mention it. . . . Except, of course, in so far as Dourlowski is concerned. . . . As for him, they haven't found him yet. . . ."

Philippe did not reply. Had he as much as heard? With short movements of his stick, he was striking the heads off the flowers that lined the road: harebells, wild thyme, gentians, angelica. Marthe remembered that this was a trick which he used to condemn in his sons.

Before coming to the pass, the road narrowed into a path that wound through the woods, clinging to the roots of the fir-trees. They climbed it one behind the other. Marthe was in front of Philippe and Suzanne. Half-way up, the path made a sudden bend. When Marthe was out of sight, Philippe felt Suzanne's hand squeeze his and hold him back.

He stopped. She nimbly pulled herself up to him:

" Philippe, you are sad. . . . It's not about me, is it? "

" No," he confessed, frankly.

" I knew it," she said, without bitterness. " So much has happened these last three days! . . . I no longer count with you."

He made no attempt at protest, for it was true. He thought of her sometimes, but in a casual way, as of a woman whom one loves, whom one covets, but whom one has no time to think about. He did not even analyze his feelings. They were mixed up with all the other troubles that overwhelmed him.

" I shall never forget you, Suzanne," he said.

"I know, Philippe. And I neither, I shall never forget you. . . . Only, I wanted to tell you this, which will give you a little happiness: Philippe, I give you my promise that I will face the life before me . . . that I will make a fresh start. . . . What I told you is happening within me. . . . I have more courage now that I . . . now that I have that memory to support me. . . . You have given me happiness enough to last me all my life. . . . I shall be what I should not have been . . . an honest woman. . . . I swear it, Philippe . . . and a good wife. . . ."

He understood that she meant to be married and he suffered at the thought. But he said to her, gently, after looking at her lips, her bare neck, her whole charming, fragrant and tantalizing person:

"Thank you, Suzanne. . . . It is the best proof of your love. . . . I thank you."

She went on to say to him:

"And then, Philippe, you see, I don't want to give my father pain. . . . Any one can feel that he has been very unhappy. . . . And the reason why I was afraid, the other morning, that Marthe might discover the truth . . . was because of him."

"You need not fear, Suzanne."

"I need not, need I?" she said. "There is no

danger of it. . . . And yet, this enquiry. . . . If
you were compelled to confess? . . ."

" Oh, Suzanne, how can you think it?"

Their eyes mingled fondly, their hands had not
parted. Philippe would have liked to speak affectionate words and especially to say how much he
hoped that she would be happy. But no words rose
to his lips save words of love; and he would
not. . . .

She gave a smile. A tear shone at the tip of her
lashes. She stammered:

" I love you. . . . I shall always love you."

Then she released her hand.

Marthe, who had turned back, saw them standing together, motionless.

When they emerged at the corner of the Albern
Path, they saw a group of journalists and sight-
seers gathered behind half-a-dozen gendarmes.
The whole road was thus guarded, as far as the
Saint-Élophe rise. And, on the right, German gen-
darmes stood posted at intervals.

They reached the Butte. The Butte is a large
round clearing, on almost level ground, surrounded
by a circle of ancestral trees arranged like the colon-
nade of a temple. The road, a neutral zone, seven
feet wide, runs through the middle.

On the west, the French frontier-post, in plain
black cast-iron and bearing a slab with directions,
like a sign-post.

On the east, the German post, in wood painted
with a black and white spiral and surmounted by
an escutcheon with the words, *" Deutsches Reich."*

Two military tents had been pitched for the
double enquiry and were separated by a space of
fifty or sixty yards.   Above each waved the flag of
its respective country.   A soldier was on guard
outside either tent: a Prussian infantryman, helmet
on head, shin-strap buckled; an Alpine rifleman,
bonneted and gaitered.   Each stood with his rifle
at the order.

Not far from them, on either side of the clearing,
were two little camps pitched among the trees:
French soldiers, German soldiers.   And the officers
formed two groups.

French and German horizons showed in the mist
between the branches.

" You see, Marthe, you see," whispered Philippe,
whose heart was gripped with emotion.   " Isn't it
terrible ? "

" Yes, yes," she said.

But a young man came towards them, carrying
under his arm a portfolio bulging with papers:

" M. Philippe Morestal, I believe ?   I am M. de
Trébons, attached to the department of the under-

secretary of state. M. Le Corbier is talking to M. Morestal your father and begs that you will be good enough to wait."

He took him, with Marthe and Suzanne, to the French camp, where they found, seated on a bench, Farmer Saboureux and Old Poussière, who had likewise been summoned as witnesses. From there, they commanded the whole circus of the Butte.

" How pale you look, Philippe!" said Marthe. " Are you ill?"

" No," he said. " Please don't worry me."

Half an hour passed. Then the canvas fly that closed the German tent was lifted and a number of persons came out.

Suzanne gave a stifled cry:

" Papa! . . . Look . . . Oh, my poor father! . . . I must go and kiss him. . . ."

Philippe held her back and she obeyed, feebly. Jorancé, besides, had disappeared, had been led by two gendarmes to the other camp; and Weisslicht the detective and his men were now being shown into the tent.

But the French tent opened, an instant after, to let old Morestal out. M. de Trébons was with him and went back with Saboureux and Old Poussière. All this coming and going seemed to take place by rule and was effected in great silence, interrupted only by the sound of the footsteps.

Morestal also was very pale. As Philippe put no question to him, Marthe asked:

"Are you satisfied, father?"

"Yes, we began all over again from the start. I gave all my explanations on the spot. My proofs and arguments have made an impression on him. He is a serious man and he acts with great prudence."

In a few minutes, M. de Trébons returned with Saboureux and Old Poussière. Farmer Saboureux continued disputing, in a state of great excitement:

"Hope they've finished this time! That makes three of them enquiring into me!. . . What do they want with me, after all? When I keep on telling everybody that I was fast asleep. . . . And Poussière too. . . . Isn't it so, Poussière, you and I saw none of it?"

And, suddenly seizing M. de Trébons by the arm, he said, in a choking voice:

"I say, there's not going to be a war, is there? Ah, no, we can't do with that! You can tell your gentry in Paris that we don't want it. . . . Oh, no, I've toiled enough as it is! War indeed! Uhlans burning everything!. . ."

He seemed terrified. His bony old hands clutched M. de Trébons' arm and his little eyes glittered with rage.

Old Poussière jerked his head and stammered:

"Oh, no! . . . The Uhlans! . . . The Uhlans!
. . ."

M. de Trébons released himself gently and made
them sit down.   Then, going up to Marthe:

"M. Le Corbier would be glad to see you,
madame, at the same time as M. Philippe Morestal.   And he also asks M. Morestal to be good
enough to come back."

The two Morestals and Marthe walked away,
leaving Suzanne Jorancé behind.

But, at that moment, a strange thing happened,
which, no doubt, had its effect on the march of
events.   From the German tent issued Weisslicht
and his men, followed by an officer in full uniform,
who crossed the open space, went up to M. de Trébons and told him that his excellency the Statthalter,
having completed his enquiries, would feel greatly
honoured if he could have a short conversation with
the under-secretary of state.

M. de Trébons at once informed M. Le Corbier,
who, escorted by the German officer, walked towards the road, while M. de Trébons showed the
Morestal family in.

The tent, which was a fairly large one, was fur-
nished with a few chairs and a table, on which lay
the papers dealing with the case.   A page lay open
bearing Saboureux's clumsy signature and the mark
made by Old Poussière.

The Morestals were sitting down, when a sound of voices struck their ears and, through the opening in the fly of the tent, they caught sight of a person in a general's uniform, very tall, very thin, looking like a bird of prey, but presenting a fine appearance in a long black tunic. With his hand on the hilt of his sword, he was striding along the road in the company of the under-secretary.

Morestal whispered:

" The Statthalter. . . . They have already had one meeting, an hour ago."

The two men disappeared at the end of the Butte, then returned and, this time, doubtless embarrassed by the propinquity of the German officers, penetrated a few paces into French territory.

A word, here and there, of the conversation reached the tent. Then the two speakers stood still and the Morestals distinctly heard the Statthalter's voice:

" Monsieur le ministre, my conclusion is necessarily different from yours, because all the police-officers who took part in the arrest are unanimous in declaring that it was effected on German soil."

" Commissary Jorancé and M. Morestal," objected M. Le Corbier, " state the contrary."

" They are alone in saying so."

" M. Philippe Morestal took the evidence of Private Baufeld."

" Private Baufeld was a deserter," retorted the Statthalter. " His evidence does not count."

There was a pause. Then the German resumed, in terms which he picked slowly and carefully:

" Therefore, monsieur le ministre, as there is no outside evidence in support of either of the two contradictory versions, I can find no argument that would tend to destroy the conclusions to which all the German enquiries have led. That is what I shall tell the emperor this evening."

He bowed. M. Le Corbier took off his hat, hesitated a second and then, making up his mind:

" One word more, your excellency. Before finally going back to Paris, I determined to call the Morestal family for the last time. I will ask your excellency if it would be possible for Commissary Jorancé to be present at the interview. I will answer for him on my honour."

The Statthalter appeared embarrassed. The proposal evidently went beyond his powers. Nevertheless, he said, decisively:

" You shall have your wish, monsieur le ministre. Commissary Jorancé is here, at your disposal."

He clapped his heels together, raised his hand to his helmet and gave the military salute. The interview was ended.

The German crossed the frontier. M. Le Corbier watched him walk away, stood for a moment in thought and then returned to the French tent.

He was surprised to find the Morestals there. But he gave a gesture as though, after all, he was rather pleased than otherwise at this accident and he asked M. de Trébons:

"Did you hear?"

"Yes, monsieur le ministre."

"Then do not lose a moment, my dear Trébons. You will find my car at the bottom of the hill. Go to Saint-Élophe, telephone to the prime minister and communicate the German reply to him officially. It is urgent. There may be immediate measures to be taken . . . with regard to the frontier."

He said these last words in a low voice, with his eyes fixed on the two Morestals, went out with M. de Trébons and accompanied him as far as the French camp.

A long silence followed upon his disappearance. Philippe, clenching his fists, blurted out:

"It's terrible . . . it's terrible. . . ."

And turning to his father:

"You are quite sure, I suppose, of what you are swearing? . . . Of the exact place? . . ."

Morestal shrugged his shoulders.

Philippe insisted:

"It was at night. . . . You may have made a mistake. . . ."

"No, no, I tell you, no," growled Morestal, angrily. "I know what I am talking about. You'll end by annoying me."

Marthe tried to interfere:

"Come, Philippe. . . . Your father is accustomed to . . ."

But Philippe caught her by the arm and, roughly:

"Hold your tongue . . . I won't allow it. . . . What do you know? . . . What are you meddling for?"

He broke off suddenly, as though ashamed of his anger, and, in a fit of weakness and uncertainty, murmured an apology:

"I beg your pardon, Marthe. . . . You too, father, forgive me. . . . Please forgive me. . . . There are situations in which we are bound to pardon one another for all the pain that we can give one another."

Judging by the contraction of his features, one would have thought that he was on the verge of crying, like a child trying to restrain its tears and failing in the effort.

Morestal stared at him in amazement. His wife looked at him aslant and felt fear rising within her, as at the approach of a great calamity.

But the tent opened once more. M. Le Corbier entered. Special Commissary Jorancé, who had been brought to the French camp by the German gendarmes, was with him.

Jorancé simply nodded to the Morestals and asked:

" Suzanne? "

" She is well," said Marthe.

Meanwhile, Le Corbier had sat down and was turning over the papers.

With his three-cornered face, ending in a short, peaked beard, his clean-shaven upper-lip, his sallow complexion and his black clothes, he wore the solemn mien of a Protestant divine. People said of him that, in the days of the Revolution, he would have been Robespierre or Saint-Just. His eyes, which expressed sympathy and almost affection, belied the suggestion. In reality, he was a conscientious man, who owed the gravity of his appearance to an excessive sense of duty.

He closed the bundles of papers and sat thinking for some time. His lips formed silent syllables. He was obviously composing his speech. And he spoke as follows, in a confidential and friendly tone which was infinitely perturbing:

" I am going back in an hour. In the train, I shall draw up a report, based on these notes and on the respective depositions which you have made

or which you will make to me. At nine o'clock
this evening, I shall be with the prime minister.
At half-past nine, the prime minister will speak
in the chamber; and he will speak according to
the substance of my report. This is what I wish
you to understand above all things. Next, I want
you to know the German reply, I want you to realize the great, the irretrievable importance of every
word which you utter. As for me, feeling as I do
the full weight of my responsibilities, I wish to
seek behind those words, beyond yourselves,
whether there is not some detail unperceived by
yourselves which will destroy the appalling truth
established by your evidence. What I am seeking
is — I tell you so frankly — a doubt on your part,
a contradiction. I am seeking it . . ."

He hesitated and, sinking his voice, concluded:
" I am almost hoping for it."

A great sense of peace filled the Morestals. Each
of them, subduing his excitement, suddenly raised
himself to the level of the task assigned to him and
each of them was ready to fulfil it courageously,
blindly, in the face of every obstacle.

And Le Corbier resumed:

" M. Morestal, here is your deposition. I ask
you for the last time to affirm the exact, complete
truth."

" I affirm it, monsieur le ministre."

" Still, Weisslicht and his men declare that the arrest took place on German soil."

" The upland widens out at this part," said Morestal, " and the road which marks the boundary winds. . . . It is possible for foreigners to make a mistake. It is not possible for us, for me. We were arrested on French soil."

" You certify this on your honour? "

" I swear it on the heads of my wife and son. I swear it to God."

Le Corbier turned to the special commissary:

" M. Jorancé, do you confirm this deposition? "

" I confirm each of my friend Morestal's words in every respect," said the commissary. " They express the truth. I swear it on the head of my daughter."

" The policemen have taken just as solemn oaths," observed Le Corbier.

" The German policemen's evidence is interested. It helps them to shield the fault which they have committed. We have committed no fault. If chance had caused us to be arrested on German territory, no power on earth would have prevented Morestal and myself from admitting the fact. Morestal is free and fears nothing. Well, I, who am a prisoner, fear nothing either."

" That is the view which the French government has adopted," said the under-secretary. " More-

over, we have additional evidence: yours, M. Philippe Morestal. That evidence the government,
through an excessive feeling of scruple, has not
wished to recognize officially. As a matter of fact,
it appeared to us less firm, more undecided, at the
second hearing than at the first. But, such as it
is, it assumes a peculiar value in my eyes, because
it corroborates that of the two other witnesses. M.
Philippe Morestal, do you maintain the terms of
your deposition, word for word?"

Philippe rose, looked at his father, pushed back
Marthe, who came running up to him, and replied,
in a low voice:

"No, monsieur le ministre."

CHAPTER VII

MARTHE ASKS A QUESTION

THE conflict was immediate. Between Morestal and Philippe, the duel set in at once. The events of the previous days had cleared the way for it: at the first word, they stood up to each other like irreconcilable adversaries, the father spirited and aggressive, the son anxious and sad, but inflexible.

Le Corbier at once foresaw a scene. He went out of the tent, ordered the sentry to stand away, made sure that the group of Germans could not hear the sound of the raised voices. Then, after carefully closing the fly, he returned to his place.

"You are mad! You are mad!" said Morestal, who had come up to his son. "How dare you?"

And Jorancé joined in:

"Come, come, Philippe . . . this is not serious. . . . You are not going to back out, to withdraw. . . ."

Le Corbier silenced them and, addressing Philippe:

"Explain yourself, monsieur," he said. "I do not understand."

Philippe looked at his father again and, slowly, in a voice which he strove to render firm as he spoke, answered:

"I say, monsieur le ministre, that certain particulars in my evidence are not accurate and that it is my duty to correct them."

"Speak, monsieur," said the under-secretary, with some harshness.

Philippe did not hesitate. Facing old Morestal, who was quivering with indignation, he began, as though he were in a hurry to get it over:

"First of all, Private Baufeld did not say things that were quite as clear as those which I repeated. The words used were obscure and incoherent."

"What! Why, your declarations are precise. . . ."

"Monsieur le ministre, when I gave my evidence for the first time before the examining-magistrate, I was under the shock of my father's arrest. I was under his influence. It seemed to me that the incident would have no consequences if the arrest had been effected on German territory; and, when relating Private Baufeld's last words, in spite of myself, without knowing it, I interpreted them in the sense of my own wishes. Later on, I understood my mistake. I am now repairing it."

He stopped. The under-secretary turned over

his papers, no doubt read through Philippe's evidence and asked:

"As far as concerns Private Baufeld, have you nothing to add?"

Philippe's legs seemed on the point of giving way beneath him, so much so that Le Corbier asked him to sit down.

He obeyed and, mastering himself, said:

"Yes, I have. I have a revelation to make in this respect which is very painful to me. My father evidently attached no importance to it; but it seems to me . . ."

"What do you mean?" cried Morestal.

"Oh, father, I beseech you!" entreated Philippe, folding his hands together. "We are not here to quarrel, nor to judge each other, but to do our duty. Mine is horrible. Do not discourage me. You shall condemn me afterwards, if you see cause."

"I condemn you as it is, Philippe."

Le Corbier made an imperious gesture and repeated, in a yet more peremptory tone:

"Speak, M. Philippe Morestal."

Philippe said, bringing the words out very quickly:

"Monsieur le ministre, Private Baufeld had relations on this side of the frontier. His desertion was prepared, backed up. He knew the safe road which he was to take."

" Through whom did he know it? "

Philippe lowered his head and, with half-closed eyes, whispered:

" Through my father! "

" That's not true! " shouted old Morestal, purple with rage. " That's not true! I prepare . . . I! . . ."

" Here is the paper which I found in Private Baufeld's pocket," said Philippe, handing a sheet of note-paper to Le Corbier. " It gives a sort of plan of escape, the road which the fugitive is to follow, the exact spot at which he is to cross the frontier so as to avoid the watchers."

" What are you saying? What are you daring to say? A correspondence between me and that wretch! "

" The two words, ' Albern Path,' are in your hand-writing, father, and it was through the Albern Path that the deserter entered France. The sheet is a sheet of your own note-paper."

Morestal gave a bound:

" And you took it from the waste-paper basket, where it lay torn and crumpled! You did a thing like that, you, my son! You had the infamy . . ."

" Oh, father! "

" Then what? Answer! "

" Private Baufeld gave it me before his death."

Morestal was standing opposite Philippe, with

his arms crossed over his chest, and, so far from defending himself against his son's accusations, seemed rather to be addressing a culprit.

And Philippe looked at him with eyes of anguish. At each blow that he struck, at each sentence that he uttered, he detected the mark of a wound on his father's face. A vein swelling on the old man's temples distressed him beyond measure. He was terrified to see streaks of blood mingle with the whites of his eyes. And he feared, at every moment, that his father would fall like a tree which the axe has struck to the heart.

The under-secretary, after examining the sheet of paper which Philippe had given him, resumed:

" In any case, M. Morestal, these lines were written by you?"

"Yes, monsieur le ministre. I have already stated what the man Dourlowski tried to get out of me and the answer which I gave him."

" Was it the first time that the fellow made the attempt? . . ."

" The first time," said Morestal, after an imperceptible hesitation.

" Then this paper? . . . These lines? . . ."

" Those lines were written by me in the course of the conversation. Upon reflection, I threw away the paper. I see now that Dourlowski must have picked it up behind my back and used it in order

to carry out his plan.   If the police had discovered
it on the deserter, it would have been a proof of
my guilt.   At least, they would have interpreted
it in that way . . . as my son does.   I hope, monsieur le ministre, that that interpretation is not
yours."

Le Corbier sat thinking for a moment or two,
consulted the documents and said:

" The two governments have agreed to leave outside the discussion all that concerns Private Baufeld's desertion, the part played by the man Dourlowski and the accusation of complicity made
against the French commissary and against yourself, M. Morestal.   These are legal questions which
concern the German courts.   The only purpose for
which I have been delegated is to ascertain whether
or not the arrest took place on French territory.
My instructions are extremely limited.   I cannot
go beyond them.   I will ask you, therefore, M.
Philippe Morestal, to tell me, or rather to confirm
to me, what you know on this subject."

" I know nothing."

A moment of stupefaction followed.   Morestal,
utterly bewildered, did not even think of protesting.   He evidently looked upon his son as mad.

" You know nothing?" said the under-secretary,
who did not yet clearly see Philippe's object.   " All
the same, you have declared that you heard M.

Jorancé's exclamation, 'We are in France! . . . They are arresting the French commissary! . . .'"

"I did not hear it."

"What! What! But you were not two hundred yards away. . . ."

"I was nowhere near. I left my father at the Carrefour du Grand-Chêne and I neither saw nor heard what happened after we had parted."

"Then why did you state the contrary, monsieur?"

"I repeat, monsieur le ministre, when my father returned, I at once understood the importance of the first words which we should speak in the presence of the examining-magistrate. I thought that, by supporting my father's story, I should be helping to prevent trouble. To-day, in the face of the inexorable facts, I am reverting to the pure and simple truth."

His replies were clear and unhesitating. There was no doubt that he was following a line of conduct which he had marked out in advance and from which nothing would make him swerve.

Morestal and Jorancé listened to him in dismay.

Marthe sat silent and motionless, with her eyes glued to her husband's.

Le Corbier concluded:

"You mean to say that you will not accept your share of the responsibility?"

"I accept the responsibility for all that I have done."

"But you withdraw from the case?"

"In so far as I am concerned, yes."

"Then I must cancel your evidence and rely upon the unshaken testimony of M. Morestal: is that it?"

Philippe was silent.

"Eh, what?" cried Morestal. "You don't answer?"

There was a sort of entreaty in the old man's voice, a desperate appeal to Philippe's better feelings. His anger almost fell, so great was his unhappiness at seeing his son, his boy, a prey to this madness.

"You mean that, don't you?" he resumed, gently. "You mean that monsieur le ministre can and must abide by my declarations?"

"No," said Philippe, stubbornly.

Morestal started:

"No? But why? What reason have you for answering like that? Why should you?"

"Because, father, though the nature of your declarations has not varied, your attitude, during the last three days, proves that you are experiencing a certain reticence, a certain hesitation."

"What makes you say that?" asked Morestal,

trembling all over, but as yet retaining his self-control.

" Your certainty is not absolute."

" How do you know? If you make an accusation, you must prove it."

" I am not making an accusation. I am trying to state my exact impression."

" Your impression! What is that worth beside the facts? And it is facts that I am asserting."

" Facts interpreted by yourself, father, facts of which you cannot be sure. No, no, you cannot! Remember, the other morning, Friday morning, we came back here and, while you were once more showing me the road which you had covered, you said, ' Still, suppose I were mistaken! Suppose we had branched off more to the right! Suppose I were mistaken!' "

" That was an exaggeration of scruple! All my acts, on the contrary, all my reflections . . ."

" There was no need to reflect! There was not even any need to return to this road! The fact that you returned to it shows that you were harassed by a doubt."

" I have not doubted for one second."

" You believe that you do not doubt, father! You believe blindly in your certainty! And you believe because you do not see clearly. You have within you a sentiment that soars above all your thoughts and all your actions, an admirable sentiment, a sentiment that makes you great: it is your love for France. You think that France is always in the right against one and all, come what may, and that she would be disgraced if she were ever in the wrong. That was the frame of mind in which you gave your evidence before the examining-magistrate. And that is the frame of mind which I ask you, monsieur le ministre, to take note of."

"And you," shouted old Morestal, bursting out at last, "I accuse you of being impelled by some horrible sentiment against your father, against your country, by I can't say what infamous ideas. . . ."

"My ideas are outside the question. . . ."

"Your ideas, which I can guess, are at the back of your conduct and of your mental aberration. If I love France too well, you, you are too ready to forget your duty to her."

"I love her as well as you do, father," cried Philippe, passionately, "and better, perhaps! It is a love that sometimes moves me to tears, when I think of what she has been, of what she is, so beautiful, so intelligent, so great, so adorable for her charm and her good faith! I love her because she is the mother of every lofty idea. I love her because her language is the clearest and noblest of all languages. I love her because she is always marching on, regardless of consequences, and because she sings as she marches and because she is gay and active and alive, always full of hopes and of illusions, and because she is the smile on the face of the world. . . . But I cannot see that she would be any the less great or admirable for admitting that one of her officials was captured twenty yards to the right of the frontier."

" Why should she admit it, if it is not true? " said Morestal.

" Why should she not admit it, if peace should be the outcome? " retorted Philippe.

" Peace! There's the great word at last! " sneered Morestal. " Peace! You too have allowed yourself to be poisoned by the theories of the day! Peace at the price of disgrace: that's it, is it not? "

" Peace at the price of an infinitesimal sacrifice of self-esteem."

" That means dishonour."

" No, no," Philippe answered, in an outburst of enthusiasm. " It is the beauty of a nation to raise itself above those miserable questions. And France is worthy of it. You do not know it, father, but since the last forty years, since that execrable date, since that accursed war the memory of which obsesses your mind and closes your eyes to every

reality of life, a new France has come into existence, a France whose gaze is fixed upon other
truths, a France that longs to shake off the evil
past, to repudiate all that remains to us of the ancient barbarism and to rid herself of the laws of
blood and war. She cannot do so yet, but she is
making for it with all her young ardour and all her
growing conviction. And twice already, in ten
years — in the heart of Africa, face to face with
England; on the shores of Morocco, face to face
with Germany — twice she has overcome her old
barbarous instinct."

"Shameful memories, for which every Frenchman blushes!"

"Glorious memories, of which we should be
proud! One day, those will be the fairest pages of
our time; and those two dates will wipe out the
execrable date. That is the true revenge! That
a nation which has never known fear, which has
always, at the tragic hours of its history, settled
its quarrels in the old barbarous fashion, sword in
hand, that such a nation should have raised itself
to so magnificent a conception of beauty and civilization, that, I say, is its finest claim to glory!"

"Words! Words! It's the theory of peace at
any price; and it is a lie that you are advising me
to tell."

"No, it is the possible truth that I ask you to admit, cruel though it may be for you to do so."

"But you know the truth," cried Morestal, waving his arms in the air. "You've sworn it three times! You've signed it three times with your name! You saw and heard the truth on the night of the attack!"

"I do not know it," said Philippe, in a firm voice. "I was not there. I was not present when you were captured and carried off. I did not hear M. Jorancé's call. I swear it on my honour. I swear it on the heads of my children. I was not there."

"Then where were you?" asked Marthe.

CHAPTER VIII

THE STAGES TO CALVARY

THE little sentence, so terrible in its conciseness, set up a clear issue between the two adversaries.

Carried away by the exuberance of their convictions, they had widened the discussion into a sort of oratorical joust in which each fought eagerly for the opinions which he held dear. And Le Corbier knew better than to interrupt a duel whence he had little doubt that some unexpected light would flash, at last, from amid the superfluous words.

Marthe's little sentence evoked that light. Le Corbier, from the beginning of the scene, had noticed the young woman's strange attitude, her silence, her fevered glances that seemed to probe Philippe Morestal's very soul. He understood the full value of the question from her accent. No more vain declamations and eloquent theories! It was no longer a matter of knowing which of the two, the father or the son, thought the more justly and served his country with the greater devotion.

One thing alone carried weight; and Marthe had stated it in undeniable fashion.

Philippe stood dumbfounded. In the course of his reflections, he had foreseen every demand, every supposition, every difficulty, in short, all the consequences of the action upon which he had resolved. But how could he have foreseen this one, not knowing that Marthe would be present at that last and greatest interview? Before Le Corbier, before his father, supposing this detail entered their heads, he could invent an excuse of some kind. But before Marthe? . . .

From that moment, he had the terrifying vision of the catastrophe that was preparing. A sweat covered his whole body. He ought to have faced the danger bravely and piled explanation on explanation at the risk of contradicting himself. As it was, he turned red and stammered. And, in so doing, he put himself out of court.

Morestal had resumed his seat. Le Corbier was waiting, impassively. Amid the great silence, Marthe, now quite pale, speaking in a slow voice, which let fall the syllables one by one, said:

"Monsieur le ministre, I accuse my husband of perjury and falsehood. It is now, when he withdraws his former evidence, that he is sinning against the truth, against a truth which he knows . . . yes,

he knows it, that I declare.   By all that he has told
me; by all that I know, I swear that he never questioned his father's word.   And I swear that he was
present at the attack."

"Then," asked Le Corbier, "why does M. Philippe Morestal act as he is doing now?"

"Monsieur le ministre," replied Marthe, "my
husband is the author of the pamphlet entitled,
Peace before All!"

The disclosure created a sort of sensation.   Le
Corbier gave a start.   The commissary wore an
indignant air.   As for old Morestal, he tried to
stand up, staggered and at once fell back in his
seat.   All his strength had left him.   His anger
gave way before an immense despair.   He could
not have suffered more had he heard that Philippe
was dead.

And Marthe repeated:

"My husband is the author of the pamphlet entitled *Peace before All!*   For the sake of his opinions, for the sake of consistency with the profound,
the exalted faith to which his views give rise within
him, my husband is capable . . ."

Le Corbier suggested:

"Of going to the length of a lie?"

"Yes," she said.   "False evidence can only appear insignificant to him beside the great catastrophe which he wishes to avert; and his conscience

alone dictates his duty to him. Is it true,
Philippe?"

He replied, gravely:

"Certainly. In the circumstances in which we
find ourselves placed, when two nations are at dag-
gers drawn over a wretched question of self-esteem,
I should not shrink from a lie that appears to me a
duty. But I have no need to resort to that expedi-
ent. I have truth itself on my side. I was not
there."

"Then where were you?" repeated Marthe.

The little sentence rang out again, pitilessly.
But, this time, Marthe uttered it in a more hostile
tone and with a gesture that underlined all its importance. And she at once added, plying him with
questions:

"You did not come in until eight o'clock in the
morning. Your bed was not undone. Consequently, you had not slept at the Old Mill. Where
did you spend the night?"

"I was looking for my father."

"You did not know that your father had been
carried off until Private Baufeld told you, at five
o'clock in the morning. Consequently, it was five
o'clock in the morning before you began to look
for your father."

"Yes."

"And, at that moment, you had not yet returned

to the Old Mill, because, I repeat, your bed was not undone."

" No."

" And where did you come from? What were you doing from eleven o'clock in the evening, when you left your father, until five o'clock in the morning, when you heard of his capture? "

The cross-examination, with its unimpeachable logic, left Philippe no loop-hole for escape. He felt that he was lost.

For a moment, he was on the point of throwing up the game and exclaiming:

" Well, yes, I was there. I heard everything. My father is right. We must accept his word. . . ."

This was a display of weakness which a man like Philippe was bound and fated to resist. On the other hand, how could he betray Suzanne?

He crossed his arms over his chest and muttered:

" I have nothing to say."

Marthe, suddenly dropping her accusing tone and shaking with anguish, rushed up to him and cried:

" You have nothing to say? What do you mean? Oh, Philippe, I entreat you, speak! . . . Confess that you are lying and that you were there . . . I beseech you. . . . My mind is full of horrible thoughts. . . . Things have been happening — I have noticed them — which obsess me now. . . . It's not true, tell me that it's not true! "

He thought that he beheld salvation in this unexpected distress. Disarmed, reduced to silence by a sort of confession which he could retract at leisure, his wife was making herself his accomplice and rescuing him by ceasing to attack him.

"You must be silent," he said, in a tone of command. "Your personal grief must make way. . . ."

"What are you saying?"

"Be silent, Marthe. We shall have the explanation which you demand. We shall have it later. But be silent."

It was a useless piece of blundering. Like all women who love, Marthe only suffered the more from this semi-avowal. She fired up in her grief:

"No, Philippe, I will not be silent. . . . I want to know what your words mean. . . . You have no right to escape by a subterfuge. . . . I demand an immediate explanation, here and now."

She had stood up and, facing her husband, emphasized each of her words with a short movement of the hand. Seeing that Philippe made no reply, Le Corbier now joined in:

"Mme. Philippe Morestal is right, monsieur. You must explain yourself and not so much for her — that is a matter between yourselves — as for me, for the purpose of the clearness of my enquiry. Ever since we began, you have kept to a sort of

programme settled in advance and easily seen
through. After denying your first depositions, you
are trying to demolish your own father's evidence.
The doubt which I was seeking behind your replies
you are now endeavouring to create in my mind by
throwing suspicion upon your father's statements
by every means in your power. I have the right to
ask myself if one of those means is not falsehood —
the word is not mine, monsieur, but your wife's —
and if the love of your opinions does not take
precedence of the love of truth."

"I am telling the truth, monsieur le ministre."

"Then prove it. Are you giving false evidence
now? Or was it on the former occasions? How
am I to know? I require a positive certainty. If
I can't have that, I shall take no notice of what you
say and rely upon the evidence of a witness who, at
any rate, has never varied."

"My father is mistaken. . . . My father is a victim of illusions. . . ."

"Until I receive a proof to the contrary, monsieur, your accusations can carry no weight with me.
They will do so only if you give me an undeniable
proof of your sincerity. Now there is only one that
would bear that undeniable character; and you refuse to supply me with it. . . ."

"But . . ."

"I tell you, monsieur," Le Corbier interrupted,

impatiently, "that there is no other question at
issue. Either you were on the frontier at the time
of the attack and heard M. Jorancé's protests, in
which case your former evidence and M. Morestal's
retain all their importance, or else you were not
there, in which case it becomes your imperative duty
to prove to me that you were not there. It is very
easy: where were you at that moment?"

Philippe had a fit of rebellion and, replying aloud
to the thoughts that tortured him:

"Ah, no!" he said. "Ah, no! . . . It's not
possible that I should be forced to. . . . Nonsense,
it would be monstrous! . . ."

It seemed to him as though a malevolent genius
had been trying, for four days past, to direct events
in such a way that he, Philippe, was under the terrible necessity of accusing Suzanne.

"No, a thousand times no!" he repeated, angrily.
"There is no power that can compel me. . . . Say
that I spent the night walking about, or sleeping by
the roadside. Say what you please. . . . But leave
me free in my actions and my words."

"In that case," said the under-secretary of state,
gathering up his papers, "the enquiry is at an end
and M. Morestal's evidence will serve as the basis
on which I shall form my conclusions."

"Very well," retorted Philippe, beside himself.

He began to walk, almost to run, around the tent.

He was like a wild animal seeking an outlet. Was he to throw up the work which he had undertaken? Was he, the frail obstacle self-set against the torrent, to be vanquished in his turn? Oh, how gladly he would have given his own life! He became aware of this, deep down in his inner consciousness. And he understood, as it were physically, the sacrifice of those who go to their death smiling, when a great idea uplifts them.

But in what respect would death have settled things? He must either speak — and speak against Suzanne: a torture infinitely more exquisite than death — or else resign himself. It was this or that: there was no alternative.

He walked to and fro, as though tormented by the fire that devoured him. Was he to fling himself on his knees before Marthe and ask for mercy or to fold his hands before Le Corbier? He did not know. His brain was bursting. And he had the harrowing feeling that all his efforts were in vain and turning against himself.

He stopped and said:

" Monsieur le ministre, your opinion alone matters; and I will attempt impossibilities to make that opinion agree with the real facts. I am prepared for anything, monsieur le ministre . . . on one condition, however, that our interview is private. To you and to you alone I can . . ."

Once more, he found Marthe facing him, Marthe, the unforeseen enemy, who seemed to hold him gripped as a prey and who, fierce and pitiless and alive to the least attempt at stratagem, would never let him go.

" I have the right to be there! " she cried.   " You must explain yourself in my presence!   Your word will have no value unless I am there. . . . If not, I shall challenge it as a fresh lie.   Monsieur le ministre, I put you on your guard against a trick. . . ."

Le Corbier gave a sign of approval and, addressing Philippe:

" What is the use of a private interview, monsieur?   Whatever credit I may attach to your confidential statements, if I am to believe them frankly I must have a check with which only your wife and your father can supply me.   Unfortunately, after all your contradictory versions, I am entitled to doubt . . ."

" Monsieur le ministre," Philippe hinted, " there are sometimes circumstances . . . facts that cannot be revealed . . . secrets of such a nature . . ."

" You lie!   You lie! " cried Marthe, maddened by the admission.   " It is not true.   A woman: is that what you mean?   No . . . no. . . . Ah, Philippe, I beseech you! . . . Monsieur le ministre, I swear to you that he is lying . . . I swear it to you . . . He is keeping up his falsehood to the bit-

ter end.   He betray me!   He love another woman!
You're lying, Philippe, are you not?   Oh, hush,
hush!"

Suddenly, Philippe felt a hand wringing his arm.
Turning round, he saw Commissary Jorancé, with
a white, threatening face, and heard him say, in
a dull voice:

"What did you mean to suggest?   Whom are
you talking about?   Oh, I'll make you answer,
trust me!"

Philippe stared at him in stupefaction.   And he
also stared at Marthe's distorted features.   And
he was surprised, for he did not think that he
had spoken words that could arouse their suspicions.

"But you are all mad!" he said.   "Come, M.
Jorancé. . . . Come, Marthe. . . . What's the mat-
ter?   I don't know what you can have understood.
. . . Perhaps it's my fault . . . I am so tired!"

"Whom have you been talking about?" repeated
Jorancé, shaking with rage.

"Confess!   Confess!" demanded Marthe, pressing him hard with all her jealous hatred.

And, behind her, Philippe saw old Morestal, huddled in his chair, as though unable to recover from
the blows that had struck him.   That was Philippe's
first victim.   Was he to offer up two more?   He
started:

"Enough! Enough! . . . This is all hateful.
. . . There is a terrible misunderstanding between
us. . . . And all that I say only makes it worse.
. . . We will have an explanation later, I promise
you, M. Jorancé. . . . You also, Marthe, I swear it.
. . . And you will realize your mistake. But let
us be silent now, please. . . . We have tortured one
another long enough."

He spoke in so resolute a voice that Jorancé stood
undecided and Marthe herself was shaken. Was
he stating the truth? Was it simply a misunderstanding that divided them?

Le Corbier guessed the tragedy and, attacking
Philippe in his turn, said:

"So, monsieur, I must look for no enlightenment
on the point to which you drew my attention? And
it is you yourself, is it not, who, by your definite
attitude, close the discussion?"

"Yes," replied Philippe, firmly.

"No," protested Marthe, returning to the charge
with indefatigable vigour. "No, it is not finished,
monsieur le ministre; it cannot finish like this. My
husband, whether he meant to or not, has uttered
words which we have all interpreted in the same
sense. If there is a misunderstanding, let it be dispelled now. And there is only one person who can
do so. That person is here. I ask to have that
person called in."

"I don't know what you mean," stammered Philippe.

"Yes, you do, Philippe. You know to whom I refer and all the proofs that give me the right to . . ."

"Silence, Marthe," commanded Philippe, beside himself.

"Then confess. If not, I swear that . . ."

The sight of M. Jorancé stayed her threat. Unaware of Suzanne's presence at the Butte-aux-Loups, Jorancé had ceased to understand; and his suspicions, aroused by Philippe's imprudence, had become gradually allayed. At the last moment, when on the point of putting her irreparable accusation into words, Marthe hesitated. Her hatred was vanquished by the sight of the father's grief.

Moreover, just then, a diversion occurred to bring about an armistice, as it were, in the midst of the implacable conflict. Le Corbier had risen hurriedly from his seat and drawn back the tent-fly. A quick step was heard outside.

"Ah, there you are, Trébons!"

And he almost ran to fetch the young man in and plied him with questions:

"Did you speak to the prime minister? What did he say?"

M. de Trébons entered the tent. But, on catching sight of the Morestal family, he turned back:

" Monsieur le ministre, I think it would be better . . ."

" No, no, Trébons.   No one here is in the way . . . on the contrary. . . . Come, what is it?   Bad news? "

" Very bad news, monsieur le ministre.   The French embassy in Berlin has been burnt down. . . ."

" Oh! " said Le Corbier.   " Wasn't it guarded? "

" Yes, but the troops were overborne by the crowd."

" Next? "

" Germany is mobilizing all her frontier armycorps."

" But in Paris?   What about Paris? "

" Nothing but riots. . . . The boulevards are overrun. . . . At this moment, the municipal guards are charging the mob to clear the approaches to the Palais-Bourbon."

" But what do they want, when all is said? "

" War."

The word rang out like a death-knell.   After a few seconds, Le Corbier asked:

" Is that all? "

" The prime minister is anxiously awaiting your return.   'Don't let him lose a minute,' he said. ' His report might spell safety.   It is my last shot. If it misses fire, I can't answer for what will happen.' And he added, ' And, even then, it may be too late.' "

The silence was really excruciating around the table, in the little space inside that tent in which the cruelest of tragedies was hurling against one another a group of noble souls united by the most loyal affection. Each of them forgot his private suffering and thought only of the horror that loomed ahead. The sinister word was echoed in all their hearts.

Le Corbier gave a gesture of despair:

" His last shot! Yes, if my report gave him an opportunity of retreating! But . . ."

He watched old Morestal, as though he were still expecting a sudden retractation. What was the good? Supposing he took it upon himself to ex- tenuate the old man's statements, Morestal was the sort of uncompromising man who would give him the lie in public. And then the government would find itself in an unenviable plight indeed!

" Well," he said, " let fate take its course! We have done our very utmost. My dear Trébons, is the motor at the cross-roads? "

" Yes, monsieur le ministre."

" Please collect the papers; we will go. We have an hour to reach the station. It's more than we want."

He picked up his hat, his coat, took a few steps

to and fro and stopped in front of Philippe. Philippe, he half thought, had perhaps not done his utmost. Philippe perhaps had still one stage to travel. But how was Le Corbier to find out? How was he to fathom that mysterious soul and read its insoluble riddle? Le Corbier knew those men endowed with the missionary spirit and capable, in furtherance of their cause, of admirable devotion, of almost superhuman sacrifice, but also of hypocrisy, of craft, sometimes of crime. What was this Philippe Morestal's evidence worth? What part exactly was he playing? Had he deliberately and falsely given rise to the suspicion of some amorous meeting? Or was he really carrying his heroism to the point of telling the truth?

Slowly, thoughtfully, as though in obedience to a new hope, Le Corbier went back to his seat, flung his motor-coat on the table, sat down and, addressing M. de Trébons:

"One second more. . . . Leave the papers. And pray bring Mlle. Suzanne Jorancé here."

M. de Trébons left the tent.

"Is Suzanne there?" asked Jorancé, in an anxious voice. "Was she there just now? . . ."

He received no reply; and he vainly scrutinized the faces, one after the other, of those whom he was questioning. During the three or four minutes that elapsed, none of the actors in the drama made the least movement. Morestal remained seated, with his head hanging on his chest. Marthe kept her eyes fixed on the opening of the tent. As for Philippe, he awaited this additional blow with anguish in his heart. The massacre was not ended. Destiny ordained that, following upon his father, upon his wife, upon Jorancé, he himself should sacrifice this fourth victim.

Le Corbier, who was watching him, was overcome with an involuntary feeling of compassion, of sympathy almost. At that moment, Philippe's sincerity seemed to him absolute and he felt inclined to abandon the test. But distrust carried the day. Absurd though the supposition might be, he had an impression that this man was capable of falsely accusing the girl in the presence of his wife, of his father and of Jorancé himself. With Suzanne present, falsehood became impossible. The test was a cruel one, but, however it was decided, it carried with it the unimpeachable certainty without which Le Corbier was unwilling to close his enquiry.

Philippe shook all over. Marthe and Jorancé rose from their seats. The tent-fly was drawn aside. Suzanne entered.

She at once gave a movement of recoil. At the first glance, at the first sight of those motionless people, she suspected the danger which her feminine instinct had already foreseen. And, deathly pale, deprived of all her strength, she dared not come forward.

Le Corbier took her hand and, gently:

"Please be seated, mademoiselle. It is possible that your evidence may be of value to us to clear up a few points."

There was only one vacant chair, next to Jorancé. Suzanne took a few steps and looked at her father, whom she had not seen since the evening at Saint-Élophe. He turned away his head. She sat down trembling.

Then Le Corbier, who was in a hurry to finish the business, walked quickly up to Philippe and said:

"It is the last time, monsieur, that I shall apply to you. In a few minutes, everything will be irrevocably ended. It depends on your good will. . . ."

But he went no further. Never had he beheld a face ravaged as Philippe's was, nor ever so great an expression of strength and energy as showed through the chaos of those distorted features. He understood that Philippe had resolved to travel the last stage. He waited, without a word.

And indeed, as though he too were eager to reach the terrible goal, Philippe spoke and said:

" Monsieur le ministre, if I tell you for certain how I spent my night, will my words have an un-impeachable value in your mind?"

His voice was almost calm. His eyes had se-lected a spot in the tent from which he no longer dared remove them, for he feared to meet Marthe's eyes, or Jorancé's, or Suzanne's.

Le Corbier replied:

" An unimpeachable value."

" Will they tend to lessen the importance of my father's statements?"

" Yes, for I shall have to weigh those statements against the words of a man whose perfect sincerity I shall no longer have cause to doubt."

Philippe was silent. His forehead oozed sweat at every pore and he staggered like a drunken man on the point of falling.

Le Corbier insisted:

" Speak without scruple, monsieur. There are circumstances in which a man must look straight before him and in which the aim to be attained must, in a measure, blind him."

Philippe continued:

" And you think, monsieur le ministre, that your report, thus modified, may have a decisive influence in Paris?"

" I say so, positively. The prime minister has allowed me to look into his secret thoughts. More-

over, I know what he is capable of doing.   If the
conclusions of my report give him a little latitude,
he will ring up the German embassy and mount the
tribune in order to bring the chamber, to bring the
country face to face with the facts as they are.   The
cabinet will fall amid a general outcry, there will
be a few riots, but we shall have peace . . . and
peace, as you, monsieur, were saying a moment ago,
peace without dishonour, at the price of an infinitesimal sacrifice of self-esteem, which will make
France greater than ever."

"Yes . . . yes . . ." said Philippe.   "But, if it
should be too late?   If it should no longer be possible to prevent anything?"

"That," said Le Corbier, "is a thing which we
cannot foretell. . . . It may, as a matter of fact,
be too late. . . ."

This was the hardest thought of all for Philippe.
Deep hollows appeared in his cheeks.   The minutes
seemed to age him like long years of sickness.   The
sight of him suggested the faces of the dying martyrs in certain primitive pictures.   Nothing short
of physical pain can thus convulse the features of
a man's countenance.   And he really suffered as
much as if he were being stretched on the rack and
burnt with red-hot pincers.   Nevertheless, he felt
that his mind remained lucid, as must be that of
the martyrs undergoing torture, and he clearly un-

derstood that, in consequence of a series of inexorable facts, he had, for a few moments — but on the most terrible conditions! — the power of perhaps . . . of perhaps saving the world from the great scourge of war.

He stiffened himself and, livid in the face, said:

"Monsieur le ministre, what my wife suspected, what you have already guessed, is the exact truth. On Monday night, while the arrest was taking place and while the two captives were being carried to Germany, I was with Suzanne Jorancé."

It was as though Jorancé, standing behind him, had been waiting for the accusation as for an attack that must be parried without delay:

"Suzanne! My daughter!" he cried, seizing Philippe by the collar of his jacket. "What are you saying, you villain? How dare you?"

Marthe had not stirred, remained as though stunned. Old Morestal protested indignantly. Philippe whispered:

"I am saying what happened."

"You lie! You lie!" roared Jorancé. "My daughter, the purest, the most honest girl in the world! Why don't you confess that you lie? . . . Confess it! . . . Confess it! . . ."

The poor man was choking. The words were caught short in his throat. His whole frame seemed to quiver; and his eyes were filled with gleams of hatred and murderous longings and anger and, above all, pain, infinite, pitiless, human pain.

And he entreated and commanded by turns:

" Confess, confess! . . . You're lying, aren't you? . . . It's because of your opinions, that's it, because of your opinions! . . . You want a proof . . . an alibi . . . and so . . ."

And, addressing Le Corbier:

" Leave me alone with him, monsieur le ministre. . . . He will confess to me that he is lying, that he is talking like that because he has to . . . or because he is mad . . . who knows? Yes, because he is mad! . . . How could she love you? Why should she? Since when? She, who is your wife's friend. . . . Get out, I know my daughter! . . . But answer, you villain! . . . Morestal, my friend, make him answer . . . make him give his proofs. . . . And you, Suzanne, why don't you spit in his face? "

He turned upon Suzanne; and Marthe, rousing herself from her torpor, went up to the girl, as he did.

Suzanne stood tottering on her feet, with averted gaze.

" Well, what's this? " roared her father. " Won't you answer either? Haven't you a word to answer to that liar? "

She tried to speak, stammered a few confused syllables and was silent.

Philippe met her eyes, the eyes of a hunted fawn, a pair of poor eyes pleading for help.

"You admit it! You admit it!" shouted Jorancé.

And he made a sudden rush at her; and Philippe, as in a nightmare, saw Suzanne flung back, shaken by her father, struck by Marthe, who, she too, in an abrupt fit of fury, demanded the useless confession.

It was a horrible and violent scene. Le Corbier and M. de Trébons interfered, while Morestal, shaking his fist at Philippe, cried:

"I curse you! You're a criminal! Let her be, Jorancé. She couldn't help it, poor thing. He is the one to blame. . . . Yes, you, you, my son! . . . And I curse you. . . . I turn you out. . . ."

The old man pressed his hand to his heart, stammered a few words more, begging Jorancé's pardon and promising to look after his daughter, then turned on his heels and fell against the table, fainting. . . .

PART III

CHAPTER I

THE ARMED VIGIL

" Ma'am! "

" What is it? What's the matter? " asked Mme. Morestal, waking with a start.

" It's I, Catherine."

" Well? "

" They have sent from the town-hall, ma'am. . . . They are asking for the master. . . . They want instructions. . . . Victor says the troops are being mobilized. . . ."

The day before, after his fainting-fit at the Butte-aux-Loups, old Morestal was carried back to the Old Mill on a litter by the soldiers of the detachment. Marthe, who came with him, flung a few words of explanation to her mother-in-law and, without paying attention to the good woman's lamentations, without even speaking to her of Philippe and of what could have become of him, ran to her room and locked herself in.

Dr. Borel was hurriedly sent for. He examined the patient, diagnosed serious trouble in the region of the heart and refused to give an opinion.

The house was at sixes and sevens during the evening and all through that Sunday night. Catherine and Victor ran to and fro. Mme. Morestal, generally so level-headed, but accustomed to bewail her fate on great occasions, nursed the sick man and issued a multiplicity of orders. Twice she sent the gardener to the chemist at Saint-Élophe.

At midnight, the old man was suffering so much that Dr. Borel was called in again. He seemed anxious and administered an injection of morphia.

There followed a few hours of comparative calm; and Mme. Morestal, although tortured at Philippe's absence and fearing that he might do something rash, was able to lie down on the sofa.

It was then that Catherine rushed into the room, at the risk of disturbing the patient's rest.

Mme. Morestal ended by bundling her off:

"Hold your tongue, can't you? Don't you see that your master's asleep?"

"They're mobilizing the troops, ma'am. . . . It's certain that we shall have war. . . ."

"Oh, don't bother us with your war!" growled the good woman, pushing her out of the room. "Boil some water for your master and don't waste your time talking nonsense."

She herself went to work at once. But all around her was a confused noise of murmurs and exclamations, coming from the terrace, the garden and the house.

Morestal woke up at nine o'clock.

" Suzanne! Where's Suzanne? " he asked, almost before he opened his eyes.

" What! Suzanne! . . ."

" Why, yes . . . why, of course, Suzanne! . . . I promised her father . . . No one has a better right to live in this house. . . . Philippe's not here, I suppose? "

He raised himself in bed, furious at the mere thought.

" He has not come in," said his wife. " We don't know where he is. . . ."

" That's all right! He'd better not come back! . . . I've turned him out. . . . And now I want Suzanne. . . . She shall nurse me . . . she alone, do you understand? . . ."

" Come, Morestal, you surely wouldn't ask . . . It's not possible for Suzanne to . . ."

But her husband's features were contracted with such a look of anger that she dared not protest further:

" As you please," she said. " After all, if you think right . . ."

She consulted Dr. Borel by telephone. He replied that the patient must on no account be thwarted. Moreover, he undertook to see the girl, to point out to her the duty that called her to the Old Mill and to overcome any reluctance on her part.

Dr. Borel himself brought Suzanne to the house at about twelve o'clock. Red with shame, her eyes swollen with tears, she submitted to Mme. Morestal's humiliating reception and took her seat by the old man's bedside.

He gave a sigh of content when he saw her:

" Ah, I'm glad! . . . I feel better already. . . . You won't leave me, will you, my little Suzanne ? "

And he fell asleep again almost at once, under the action of a fresh injection of morphia.

As on the previous evening, the dining-room at the Old Mill remained empty. The maid took a light meal on a tray to Mme. Morestal and, next, to Marthe. But Marthe did not even answer her knock.

Marthe Morestal had not left her room during the morning; and all day she stayed alone, with her door bolted and her shutters closed. She sat on the edge of a chair and, bent in two, held her fists to her jaws and clenched her teeth so as not to scream aloud. It would have done her good to cry; and she sometimes thought that her suffering was about to find an outlet in sobbing; but the re-

lief of tears did not come to moisten her eyes.
And, stubbornly, viciously, she went over the whole
pitiful story, recalling Suzanne's stay in Paris, the
excursions on which Philippe used to take the young
girl and from which they both returned looking so
happy and glad, their meeting at the Old Mill, Philippe's departure for Saint-Élophe and, the next day,
Suzanne's strange attitude, her ambiguous questions,
her spiteful smile, as of a rival endeavouring to hurt
the wife and hoping to supplant her. Oh, what a
cruel business! And how hateful and wicked life,
once so sweet, now seemed to her!

At six o'clock, driven by hunger, she went down
to the dining-room. As she came out, after eating
a little bread and drinking a glass of water, she
saw Mme. Morestal going down the front-door steps
to meet the doctor. She then remembered that her
father-in-law was ill and that she had not yet seen
him. His bedroom was close by. She crossed the
passage, knocked, heard a voice — the voice of a
nurse, she thought — say " Come in," and opened
the door.

Opposite her, at a few steps' distance, beside the
sleeping man, was Suzanne.

" You! You! " fumed Marthe. " You here!
. . ."

Suzanne began to tremble under her fixed gaze
and stammered:

" It was your father-in-law . . . He insisted . . .
The doctor came . . ."

And, with her knees giving way beneath her, she
said, over and over again:

" I beg your pardon. . . . Forgive me . . . forgive me. . . . It was my fault. . . . Philippe would
never have . . ."

Marthe at first listened without stirring. Perhaps she might have been just able to restrain herself. But, at the name of Philippe, at the name
of Philippe uttered by Suzanne, she gave a bound,
clutched the girl by the throat and flung her back
against the table. She quivered with rage like an
animal that at last holds its foe. She would have
liked to destroy that body which her husband had
clasped in his arms, to tear it, bite it, hurt it, hurt it
as much as she could.

Suzanne gurgled under the onslaught. Then,
losing her head, Marthe, stiff-fingered, clawed her
with her nails on the forehead, on the cheeks, on
the lips, those moist, red lips which Philippe had
kissed. Her hatred gained new life with every
movement. Blood flowed and mingled with Suzanne's tears. Marthe vilified her with abominable
words, words which she had never spoken before.
And, drunk with rage, thrice she spat in her
face.

She ran out of the room, turned back, hissed a

parting insult, slammed the door and went down the
passage, calling:

"Victor!   Catherine!"

Once in her room, she pressed the bell-push until
the servants came:

"My trunk!   Bring it down!   And get the carriage ready, Victor, do you hear?   At once! . . ."

Mme. Morestal appeared, attracted by the noise.
Dr. Borel was with her.

"What's the matter, Marthe?   What is it?"

"I refuse to stay here another hour!" retorted
Marthe, heedless of the presence of the doctor and
the servants.   "You can choose between Suzanne
and me. . . ."

"My husband promised . . ."

"Very well.   As you choose that woman, I am
going."

She opened the drawers of the chest and flung
the dresses and linen out promiscuously.   With an
abrupt movement, she pulled the cloth from the
table.   All the knicknacks fell to the floor.

Dr. Borel tried to argue with her:

"This is all very well, but where are you going?"

"To Paris.   My boys will come to me there."

"But haven't you seen the papers?   The position
is growing more serious every hour.   The frontier-
corps are being mobilized.   Are you sure of getting
through?"

" I am going," she said.

" And suppose you don't reach Paris? "

" I am going," she repeated.

" What about Philippe? "

She shrugged her shoulders. He understood that nothing mattered to her, neither her husband's existence nor the threat of war, and that there was no fighting against her despair. Nevertheless, as he went away with Mme. Morestal, he said, loud enough for Marthe to hear:

" By the way, don't be uneasy about Philippe. He has been to see me and to enquire after his father. He will come back. I promised to let him know how things were going. . . ."

When Victor came, at seven o'clock, to say that the carriage was ready, Marthe had changed her mind. The thought that Philippe was hanging about the neighbourhood, that he might return to the house, that Suzanne and he would stay under the same roof and see each other as and when they pleased was more than she could bear. She remained, therefore, but standing behind her door, with her ears pricked up to catch the first sound. When everybody had gone to bed, she went downstairs and hid herself, until break of day, in a recess in the entrance-hall. She was prepared to spring out at the least creak on the stair, for she felt convinced that Suzanne would slip out in the dark with the object of joining Philippe. This time, Marthe would have killed her. And her jealousy was so exasperated that she lay in wait, not with fear, but with the fierce hope that Suzanne was really going to appear before her.

Fits such as these, which are abnormal in a woman like Marthe, who, at ordinary times, obeyed her reason more readily than her instinct, fits such as these do not last. Marthe ended by suddenly bursting into sobs. After crying for a long time, she went up to her room and, worn out with fatigue, got into bed.

That morning, on the Tuesday, Philippe came to the Old Mill. Mme. Morestal was told and hurried down, in a great state of excitement, eager to vent her wrath upon her unworthy son. But, at the sight of him standing outside on the terrace, she overcame her need of recrimination and uttered no reproach, so frightened was she at seeing him look so pale and sad.

She asked:

" Where have you been? "

" What does it matter? " replied Philippe. " I ought not to have come back . . . but I could not keep away, because of father. . . . I was too much upset. . . . How is he? "

" Dr. Borel won't say anything definite yet."

" And what is your opinion? "

" My opinion? Well, frankly speaking, I am very hopeful. Your father is so strong! But, all the same, it was a violent shock. . . ."

" Yes," he said, " that is what alarms me. I have not lived, these last two days. How could I possibly go before knowing for certain? . . ."

She hinted, with a certain feeling of apprehension:

" Then you want to stay here? "

" Yes . . . provided he does not know."

" The fact is . . . it's like this . . . Suzanne is here, in your father's room. . . . He insisted on her coming. . . ."

" Oh! " he said. " Is Suzanne here? "

" Where would you have her go? She has no one left. Who knows when Jorancé will be out of prison? And, besides, will he ever forgive her? "

He stood wrapped in thought and asked:

" Has Marthe met her? "

" There was a terrible scene between them. I found Suzanne with her face streaming with blood, all over scratches."

" Oh, the poor things! " he murmured. " The poor things! . . ."

His head fell; and, presently, she saw that he was weeping.

As she had no word of consolation to offer him, she turned round and walked to the drawing-room, where she shifted the furniture so as to have the satisfaction of putting it back in its place. She tried to find a pretext to utter her resentment. When Philippe sat down at the table, she showed him the newspapers:

" Have you seen them? "

" Yes, the news is bad."

" That's not the point. The point is that the cabinet has fallen on the publication of the under-secretary's report. The whole Chamber rose up in protest."

" Well? "

" Well, that report is the one based upon the last enquiry . . . of two days ago . . . at the Butte-aux-Loups. . . . So you see . . ."

Philippe felt a need to justify himself:

" You forget, mother, that there was an unexpected factor in the case. Before the sitting of the Chamber, a telegram had been published reporting the words spoken by the emperor after hearing the Statthalter's explanation."

He pointed to one of the papers:

" Here, mother, read this. These are the emperor's own words: ' Our conscience is now at ease. We had the might; we have the right. God decide the issue! I am ready.' And the Chamber, when condemning and overthrowing a ministry that was prepared for conciliation, intended to reply to words which it looked upon as provocative."

"Very well," said the old lady. "But, all the same, the report made no difference."

"Yes, that is so."

"Then what was the good of all your fuss and bothering? It was no use doing so much harm, considering that it served no purpose."

Philippe shook his head:

"It had to be. Certain actions must be performed and they should not be judged by the consequences which accident thrusts upon them, but by those which we expected of them, in all human logic and in all good faith."

"Empty phrases!" she said, obstinately. "You ought not to have done it. . . . It was a very useless piece of heroism. . . ."

"Don't think that, mother. There was no need to be a hero to act as I did. It was enough to be an honest man. No one with the same clear vision as myself of what might happen would have hesitated any more than I did."

"So you regret nothing?"

He took her hand and, sadly:

"Oh, mother, how can you talk like that, you who know me? How can I be indifferent to all this break-up around me?"

He spoke the words with such despondency that she received an insight into his distress. But her anger with him was too great and especially their natures were too different for her to be touched by it. She concluded:

" No matter, my boy, it's all your fault. If you had not listened to Suzanne. . . ."

He did not reply. The accusation cut into the most sensitive part of a wound which nothing could allay; and he was not the man to seek excuses.

" Come," said his mother.

She took him to another room on the second floor, further than the first from that which Marthe occupied:

" Victor will bring you your bag and serve your meals in here; that will be best. And I will let your wife know."

" Give her this letter, which I got ready for her," he said. " It is only asking for an interview, an explanation. She can't refuse."

In this way, in the course of that Tuesday, the Morestal family were once more gathered under the same roof; but in what heart-rending conditions! And how great was the hatred that now divided those beings once united by so warm an affection!

Philippe felt the disaster in a way that was, so to speak, visible and palpable, during these hours in which each of his victims remained locked up, as though in a torture-chamber. Nothing could have distracted his mind from its obsession, and even the fear of that accursed war which he had not been able to avert.

And yet news reached him at every moment, threatening news, like the news of a plague that comes nearer and nearer, despite the distance, despite the intervening waters.

At lunch-time, it was Victor, who had hardly entered the room with Philippe's tray before he exclaimed:

" Have you heard of the telegram from England, sir? The British premier has declared in parliament that, if war came, he would land a hundred thousand men at Brest and Cherbourg. That means an open alliance."

Later on, he heard the gardener's son, Henriot, returning on his bicycle from Saint-Élophe, shouting to his father and Victor:

" There's a mutiny at Strasburg! They're barricading the streets! They've blown up one of the barracks!"

And Victor at once telephoned to the *Éclaireur des Vosges,* pretending that he was doing so on behalf of M. Morestal, and came running up to Philippe's room:

"M. Philippe, Strasburg is in a state of insurrection. . . . All the peasants of the country around have taken up arms."

And Philippe reflected that there was no hope, that the governments would have their hands forced. And he reflected upon it almost calmly. His part was played. Nothing interested him now but his personal sorrow, the health of his father, the sufferings of Marthe and Suzanne, those first victims of the hateful scourge.

At five o'clock, he heard that one of the countries had issued an ultimatum against the other. Which of the two countries? And what was the purport of the ultimatum? He was unable to learn.

At nine o'clock, the telegrams announced that the new cabinet, chosen for the greater part from among the members of the opposition, had moved the immediate creation of "a Committee of National Safety, charged to take all the necessary measures for the defence of the country in case of war." The Chamber had passed the motion through its various stages in one sitting and had appointed the Governor of Paris head of the Committee of National Safety, with discretionary powers. This implied an eventual dictatorship.

All that Tuesday night, the Old Mill, silent and gloomy within doors, was filled with noise and excitement from without, a prey to the fever that precedes great catastrophes. Victor, the gardener and the gardener's son by turns bicycled at full speed to Saint-Élophe, where other people were bringing news from the sub-prefecture. The women moaned and wailed. At three o'clock in the morning, Philippe distinguished the angry voice of Farmer Saboureux.

At daybreak, there was a lull. Philippe, exhausted by so many sleepless nights, ended by dozing off and, while still asleep, heard the sound of footsteps coming and going over the pebbles in the garden. Then, suddenly, pretty late in the morning, he was awakened by a clamour outside.

He sprang out of bed. In front of the steps, Victor leapt from his horse, shouting:

" The ultimatum is rejected. It's war. It's war ! "

CHAPTER II

PHILIPPE went downstairs as soon as he was dressed. He found all the servants gathered in the hall, discussing the news. Victor confirmed it: he had come straight from Noirmont.

Moreover, the postman had heard from a gendarme that the railway-station at the sub-prefecture was occupied by soldiers. He himself, when he left Saint-Élophe, had seen army telegraphists on duty in the post-office.

These hasty measures fitted in with the rejection of the ultimatum and went to prove the imminence of the dreaded catastrophe.

Philippe could not help saying:

" That means war."

" It's what I've been shouting from the house-tops for the last two days! " proclaimed Victor, who seemed greatly excited. " Oughtn't we to make preparations, here? At two steps from the frontier? "

But a bell rang. Catherine ran to the drawing-room, where Mme. Morestal appeared:

" Where were you? I have been looking for you. Hasn't the doctor been? Oh, there you are, Philippe! Quick, telephone to the doctor. . . ."

" Is my father . . .? "

" Your father is better; but, all the same, he's sleeping longer than he ought. . . . It may be the morphia. . . . You had better telephone."

She left the room. Philippe was taking down the receiver, when some one tapped him on the shoulder. It was Victor, whose excitement was increasing every moment and who asked him with a perplexed air:

" What are we to do, M. Philippe? Are we going to stay here? Or go away and shut up the house? The mistress does not realize . . ."

And, without waiting for the answer, he turned round:

" Isn't it so, Catherine, the mistress does not realize . . . The master's quite well again. . . . Well, then, they should make up their minds! . . ."

" Of course, one must be prepared for everything," said the maid-servant. " Suppose the enemy invade us? "

They both of them walked up and down the drawing-room, opening the doors, shutting them again, making gestures through the window.

An old woman entered, an old woman who was

employed at the Old Mill as a charwoman. She
waved her arms about:

" Is it true? Is it true? Are we going to war?
And my son, the youngest, who is with his regiment? . . . And the other, who is in the reserve?
. . . Is it true? No, tell me it's not true! It's all
nonsense they're talking! "

" Nonsense, indeed! " said the gardener's wife,
appearing on the scene. " You'll soon see if it's
nonsense! . . . They'll all have to go . . . my husband too, who's in the reserve of veterans."

She was accompanied by a child of three or four
years old and in her arms carried another, in swad-
dling-clothes, who was whimpering.

" Of course they'll have to go," said Victor.
" And what about me? You'll see, they'll call me
to the colours, though I'm past the age! . . . You'll
see! . . ."

" You as well as the rest," grinned the gardener,
who now entered in his turn. " As long as one can
hold a rifle. . . . But our eldest, Henriot, who's sixteen: do you think they'll forget him? "

" Oh, as for him," scolded the mother, " I shall
hide him if they try to take him from me! "

" And what about the gendarmes? "

All were gesticulating and talking together. And
Victor repeated:

"Meantime, we had better be off. Shut up the house and go. That's the wisest. We can't remain here like this, at two steps from the frontier."

In his eyes, war represented the disordered flight of the old men and the women, running away in herds and pushing before them carts loaded with furniture and bedding. And he stamped his foot, resolved upon making an immediate move.

But a great hullabaloo arose on the terrace. A little farm-labourer came rushing into the drawing-room:

"He's seen some! He's seen some!"

He was running in front of his employer, Farmer Saboureux, who arrived like a whirlwind, with his eyes starting out of his head:

"I've seen some! I've seen some! There were five of them! I've seen some!"

"Seen what? Seen what?" said Victor, shaking him. "What have you seen?"

"Uhlans!"

"Uhlans! Are you sure?"

"As I see you now! There were five of them on horseback! Oh, I knew them again . . . it wasn't the first time! . . . Uhlans, I tell you! . . . They'll burn everything down!"

Mme. Morestal came running up at the noise which he made:

" Do be quiet! What's the matter with you? "

" I've seen some! " yelled Saboureux. " Uhlans! They've gone off to fetch the others."

" Uhlans! " she gasped in dismay.

" Yes, like last time! "

" Oh, heaven! Is it possible? "

" I saw them, I say. . . . Go and tell monsieur le maire."

She lost her temper:

" Tell him? But he's ill! . . . And be quiet, you, I've had enough of it. . . . Philippe, is the doctor coming? "

Philippe put down the telephone:

" The line is engaged by the military, it's not available for private communications."

"Oh, but this is terrible! " said the old lady. ' What's to become of us? "

She thought only of Morestal, confined to his room, and of the inconvenience which he would suffer through this state of things.

A bicycle-bell was heard outside.

" Ah! " cried the gardener, leaning out of the window on the garden side. " There's my boy coming. . . . How the rascal is growing! And you think, mother, that they'll leave him at home to pluck the geese? A sharp lad like that? . . ."

A few seconds later, the boy was in the drawing-room. Breathless, staggering, he reeled back against the table and blurted out, in a hollow voice:

" It's . . . war! . . ."

Philippe, who retained some hope in spite of everything, flew at him:

" War? "

" Yes . . . it's declared. . . ."

" By whom? "

" They didn't say."

And Saboureux, seized with fresh anger, stuttered:

"Of course! . . . I said so! . . . I saw the Uhlans . . . there were five of them."

There was a stir among the servants. All rushed to meet a new arrival, Gridoux, the official gamekeeper, who came prancing along the terrace, brandishing a stick. He pushed them aside:

" Don't bother me! . . . I've a message to give! Where's monsieur le maire? He must come at once! They're waiting for him! "

He seemed furious at not finding the Mayor of Saint-Élophe there, ready to go back with him.

" Not so loud, not so loud, Gridoux," Mme. Morestal ordered. " You'll wake him up."

" He's got to be woke up. I've been sent from the town-hall. . . . He's got to come at once."

Philippe laid hold of him:

" Stop that noise, I tell you, hang it all! My father is ill."

" That doesn't matter. I've got the butcher's cart.
. . . I'll take him with me straight away, as he
is."

" But it's impossible," moaned Mme. Morestal.
" He's in bed."

" That doesn't matter. . . . There's orders to be
given . . . There's a whole company of soldiers
. . . soldiers from the manœuvres. . . . The town-
hall is upside down. . . . He's the only one to put
things right."

" Nonsense! Where are his deputies? Arnauld?
Walter?"

" They've lost their heads."

" Who's at the town-hall?"

" Everybody."

" The parish-priest?"

" A milksop!"

" The parson?"

" An ass! There's only one man who isn't crying
like the others. . . . But M. Morestal would never
consent . . . They're not friends."

" Who is that?"

" The school-master."

" Let them obey him, then! . . . The school-master will do! . . . Let him give orders in my husband's name."

The wish to save Morestal any annoyance gave
her a sudden authority.   And she pushed everybody
out, to the stairs, to the hall:

" There, go away, all of you. . . . Gridoux, go
back to the town-hall. . . ."

" Yes, that's it," said Saboureux, gripping the
gamekeeper's arm, " go back to Saint-Élophe,
Gridoux, and send the soldiers to me, eh?   Let them
defend me, hang it all!   The Uhlans will burn down
everything, my house, my barn! "

They all went out in high excitement.   Philippe
was able for a long time to distinguish Farmer Saboureux's exclamations through the garden window.
And the picture of all those anxious, noisy people,
drunk with talk and action, rushing from side to
side in obedience to unreasoning impulses, that picture suggested to him a vision of the great mad
crowds which the war was about to let loose like the
waves of a sea.

" Come on," he said.   " It's time to act."

He took a railway-guide from the table and turned
up the station at Langoux.   The new strategic line
passed through Langoux, the line which follows the
Vosges and runs down to Belfort and Switzerland.
He found that he could reach Bâle and sleep at
Zurich that same evening.

He stood up and looked around him, with his heart
wrung at the thought of going away like that, with-

out bidding good-bye to any one.   Marthe had not
answered his letter and remained invisible.   His
father had turned him out and would never forgive
him.   He must go away by stealth, like a malefactor.
" Well," he murmured, thinking of the act which he
was on the point of accomplishing, " it's better so.
In any case and in spite of everything, I was bound,
now that war has been declared, to appear a mis-
creant and a renegade in my father's eyes.   Have
I the right to rob him of the least affectionate
word? "

Mme. Morestal came up from the garden and he
heard her moaning:

" War!   Oh, heaven, war, like last time!   And
your poor father forced to keep his bed!   Ah, Philippe, it's the end of all things! "

She shifted a few chairs in their places, wiped
the table-cover with her apron and, when the drawing-room seemed tidy to her eyes, went to the
door:

" Perhaps he is awake. . . . What will he want
to do, when he hears? . . . If only he keeps quiet!
A man of his age . . ."

Philippe went up to her, in an instinctive burst of
confidence:

" You know I'm going, mother? "

She replied:

" You're going?   Well, yes, you are right.   I

dare say I shall persuade Marthe to come back to
you. . . ."

He shook his head:

" I'm afraid not. . . ."

" Yes, yes," she declared, " Marthe loves you very
much.   And then there are the children to bring you
together.   Leave it to me. . . . The same with your
father: don't be alarmed. . . . Everything will
smooth down in time between the two of you.   Go,
my boy. . . . Write to me often. . . ."

" Won't you kiss me, mother? "

She kissed him on the forehead, a quick, cold kiss
that revealed her lingering bitterness.

But, as she was opening the door, she stopped, reflected and said:

" You are going back to Paris, are you not?   To
your own place? "

" Why do you ask, mother? "

" An idea that came to me, that's all.   My head
is in such a state, because of your father, that I did
not think of it before. . . ."

" What idea?   Can you tell me? "

" About this war . . . But, no, as a professor,
you're exempt, aren't you? "

He understood her fears and, as he was unable to
reassure her by confessing his secret intentions, he
did not enlighten her further:

" Yes," he said, " I'm exempt."

" Still, you spent some time in the reserve? "

" Only at the government offices. And that's where we serve in time of war."

" Oh," she said, " that's all right, that's all right! . . . Else I should have been very anxious. . . . You see, the mere thought that you might be fighting . . . that you might be wounded . . . oh, it would be horrible! "

She drew him to her with a sort of violence that delighted Philippe and kissed him as he had longed to be kissed. He was nearly saying:

" Do you understand, mother darling? . . . Do you understand what I was trying to do, the other day? Thousands and thousands of mothers will be made to shed tears. . . . Great as our private troubles are, they will pass. Those which begin to-morrow will never pass. Death is irreparable."

But why waste words? Did not his mother's emotion prove him absolutely right?

They remained for a few moments locked in each other's embrace and the old lady's tears fell upon Philippe's cheeks.

At last, she said:

" You are not going at once, are you? "

" As soon as I have packed my bag."

" What a hurry you are in! Besides, there's no train yet. No, I want to kiss you once more and to make sure that you have all you want. And then

it's impossible for you and Marthe to part like this.
I will speak to her presently. But I must go to your
father first: he may want me. . . ."

He went with her as far as the sick man's room
and, as she had taken from a cupboard a pile of tow-
els that filled her arms, she said:

" Open the door for me, will you? "

Then he saw his father at the other end of the
room, lying lifeless, very pale in the face, and Suzanne sitting at the foot of the bed. He clearly distinguished the red scratches on her cheeks and chin.

" Shut the door, Suzanne," said Mme. Morestal,
when she was inside.

Suzanne did so. As she approached, she saw
Philippe in the dusk of the passage. She did not
make a movement nor give a start; and she closed
the door upon him as though he had not been there.

" She too," thought Philippe, " she too will never
forgive me, any more than my father or Marthe."

And he resolved to go away at once, now that
his mother's affection had given him a little comfort.

He found Victor at the foot of the garden-steps,
indulging in lamentations in the midst of the other
servants and recommending immediate flight:

" We can pack up the plate, the clocks, the valua-
bles in an hour and be off. . . . When the enemy
arrive, they will find no one here. . . ."

Philippe called him and asked if it was possible to get a carriage at Saint-Élophe:

"Oh, are you going, sir? You are quite right. But not just yet, are you? Presently, I suppose, with Mme. Philippe? I've orders to drive Mme. Philippe to Saint-Élophe. From there, there's the diligence that goes to Noirmont."

"No, I am not going in that direction."

"How do you mean, sir? There's only one line to Paris."

"I sha'n't go straight to Paris. I want to take the train at Langoux."

"The new line to Switzerland? But that's an endless journey, sir! It goes all the way down to Belfort."

"Yes, that's it. How far is it from Saint-Élophe to Langoux?"

"Three miles and a bit."

"In that case, I shall walk," said Philippe. "Thank you."

He was in a hurry to leave the Old Mill, for he felt that events were hastening to a crisis and that, at any moment, he might be prevented from carrying out his plan.

As a matter of fact, when he turned back, he was passed by Henriot, the gardener's son, who was clapping his hands:

"There they are! The soldiers of the manœuvring company! . . . They are going to the Col du Diable, at the quick step. We shall see them from the terrace."

He was followed by the other servants, by his mother, by his little brother, who, like himself, was waving his hands; and they all crossed the drawing-room.

Philippe went to the edge of the terrace. The troops were already debouching in good order. They were young soldiers, beardless boys for the most part, and looked almost like children amusing themselves by marching in file. But he saw an un-accustomed expression of anxiety and doubt on their faces. They marched in silence, hanging their heads and as though bent by the fatigue of the recent manœuvres.

A word of command sounded in the rear and was repeated in a sharp voice by two non-commissioned officers. There was a momentary undulating movement. Then the column proceeded at the double down the slope that led to the Étang-des-Moines.

And, when the last ranks had filed off below the terrace, two officers appeared, followed by a bugler. One of the two sprang briskly from his horse, flung the reins to the bugler and ran up the staircase, shouting:

" I'll be with you presently, Fabrègues. . . . Meet

me in the Col du Diable. . . . Take up your position
at Saboureux's Farm."

On reaching the terrace, he raised his hand to his
cap:

" Can I see M. Morestal, please? "

Philippe stepped forward:

" My father is laid up, captain."

The officer was obviously affected by the news:

" Oh! " he said. " I was relying on M. Morestal.
I have had the pleasure of making his acquaintance
and he spoke to me of the Old Mill. . . . I now
see what he meant. The position is really excellent.
But, for the moment, monsieur, would you mind?
. . . I know you are on the telephone here and I
have an urgent message. . . . Excuse me . . . it is
such a serious time. . . ."

Philippe took him to the telephone. The officer
pressed the button impatiently and, as he did not
receive a reply at once, turned round:

" Meanwhile, allow me to introduce myself . . .
Captain Daspry. . . . I met your father in con-
nection with a rather funny incident, the slaughter
of Farmer Saboureux's fowls. . . . Hullo! Hullo!
Gad, how difficult it is to get put on! . . . Hullo!
Hullo! . . . I even shocked M. Morestal by refus-
ing to punish the culprit, one Duvauchel, an incor-
rigible anti-militarist. . . . An excuse like that
would just have served the beggar's turn. . . ."

He had a rather vulgar type of face and a complexion that was too red; but his frank eyes and his gaiety of manner made him exceedingly attractive. He began to laugh:

"To show his gratitude, Duvauchel promised me, this morning, to turn his back on the enemy, at the first shot, and to desert. . . . He has a chauffeur's place reserved for him in Switzerland. . . . And, as Duvauchel says, ' There's nothing like a French greaser.' . . . Hullo! . . . Ah, at last! . . . Hullo! Captain Daspry speaking. . . . I want the military post at Noirmont. . . . Yes, at once, please. . . . Hullo! . . . Is that Noirmont? The military post? I want Major Dutreuil. . . . Switch me on to him. . . . It's urgent."

Captain Daspry ceased. Instinctively, Philippe took up the other receiver:

"May I?"

"Oh, certainly! . . ."

And Philippe heard the following dialogue, with its swift and anxious questions and answers:

"Is that you, Daspry?"

"Yes, major."

"Did the cyclists catch you up?"

"Which cyclists?"

"I sent three after you."

"I've seen nothing of them so far. I'm at Morestal's."

" The Old Mill? "

" Yes, major . . . I wrote to you about it."

" Well, what is it, Daspry? "

" Uhlans have been seen in the Col du Diable."

" Yes, I know. The Börsweiler cavalry are on the march."

" What! "

" They will cross the frontier in an hour from now, supported by two regiments of infantry."

" What! "

" That's what I sent my cyclists to tell you. Get to the Col du Diable as fast as you can."

" My men are there, major. As soon as the enemy arrives, we will fall back, keeping in touch with them as we do so."

" No."

" Eh? But I can't do otherwise, I have only my company."

" You must stand your ground, Daspry. You must stand your ground for two hours and a half or three hours. My battalion has just left barracks. The 28th are following us by forced marches. We shall be at the frontier by two o'clock in the afternoon. You must stand your ground."

" But I say, major! "

" You must stand your ground, Daspry."

With a mechanical movement, the officer drew himself up, brought his heels together and replied:

"We shall stand our ground, major."

He replaced the receiver and thought for a few minutes. Then he said, with a smile:

"By Jove, that's a nice beginning! Two hundred men against some thousands . . . for three hours! If one of the 4th company remains alive, he'll be a lucky man. . . ."

"But it's madness!" Philippe protested.

"Monsieur, the Alpine Rifles and the 28th of the line are on their way; and Dornat's division is certainly behind them. If they arrive too late, if the ridges of the Vosges are taken, if the frontier is crossed, if the Saint-Élophe valley is occupied and all this on the very day on which war is declared, you can imagine the consternation which this first check will produce all over France. If, on the other hand, a handful of men sacrifice themselves . . . and *succeed*, the moral effect will be incalculable. I shall stand my ground for three hours, monsieur."

The words were spoken simply, with the profound conviction of a man who realizes the full importance of his act. He was already on his way down the stone steps. Saluting Philippe, he added:

"You can congratulate M. Morestal, monsieur. He is a far-seeing Frenchman. He foresaw everything that is happening. Let us hope that it is not too late."

He leapt into the saddle, spurred his horse and set off at a gallop.

Philippe followed him with his eyes as far as the Étang-des-Moines. When the officer had disappeared behind a dip in the ground, he gave way to an angry movement and muttered:

" Play-acting! "

However, he turned the telescope on the Col du Diable and saw soldiers all around Saboureux's Farm, running, scrambling up the rocks on every side with the agility of young goats. He reflected that they had forgotten their weariness and seemed to be diverting themselves with an exercise to which each contributed his own effort, his individual tactics and his qualities of self-reliance and initiative.

He stood pensive for a few minutes. But time was pressing. He called Victor and went up to his room:

" Quick, my bag."

They stuffed the papers and manuscripts into it promiscuously, together with a little linen and the toilet-articles. The bag was strapped up. Philippe seized it:

" Good-bye, Victor. Tell my mother I sent her my love."

He crossed the landing. But some one darted out of an adjacent room. It was Marthe. She barred his way:

" Where are you going? " she asked.

CHAPTER III

IDEAS AND FACTS

MARTHE, who had kept her room since the day before, but remained attentive to all that was happening at the Old Mill, had, through her open door and window, heard and seen the hubbub, the fuss made by the servants, all the mad fluster of a house that feels itself threatened by an approaching cyclone.

She had overcome her fit of anger and hatred, was now mistress of herself and was no longer frightened of a possible meeting between Philippe and Suzanne. Another torment obsessed her. What did her husband mean to do? Brought face to face with an eventuality which he had often contemplated, what line of conduct would he pursue?

And it was he that she was watching. Before she went away, she wished to know. She overheard his first conversation with Victor. She saw his meeting with Captain Daspry from a distance. She saw him go to his room. She saw him come out again. And, in spite of herself, although urged by a very definite feeling, she stood up before him like an obstacle:

"Where are you going?" she asked.

Philippe did not lose countenance.   He replied:

"What interest can that have for you?"

"Come," she said, "we have to speak to each other. . . . Come in here."

She took him into her room, shut the door and repeated, in a masterful tone:

"Where are you going, Philippe?"

He replied, with the same decision:

"I am going away."

"There is no carriage."

"I shall walk."

"Where to?"

"To Noirmont."

"To take which train?"

"The train to Paris."

"That's not true," she said, vehemently.   "You are not going to Paris.   You are going to Langoux, to take the train to Belfort."

"Just so, but I shall be in Paris to-morrow morning."

"That's not true!   You do not mean to stop at Belfort.   You will go on to Bâle, to Switzerland. And, if you go to Switzerland, it will not be for a day, it will be for months . . . for your life!"

"And what then?"

" You intend to desert, Philippe."

He did not speak. And his silence dumbfounded her. Violent as was the certainty that filled and angered her, Marthe was stupefied when he made no protest.

She stammered:

" Is it possible? You really intend to desert? "

Philippe grew irritable:

" Well, what has it to do with you? You had a letter from me yesterday, offering you an explanation. You have not even troubled to reply! Very well! I have done you an irreparable wrong. Our whole married life is shattered by my fault. Your attitude up to the present shows me that you never mean to forgive me. . . . Then what right have you to call me to account for what I do? "

She repeated, in a low voice, with fixed eyes:

" You intend to desert. . . ."

" Yes."

" Is it really credible? I knew your ideas against war . . . all the ideas in your books . . . which agree with my own. . . . But I never thought of this. . . . You never spoke to me of it. . . . And then, no . . . I could never have believed it. . . ."

" You will have to believe it, for all that, Marthe."

He turned to the door. Once again she stood up in front of him.

"Let me pass," he said.

"No."

"You are mad!"

"Listen to me . . . Philippe. . . ."

"I refuse to listen. This is not the time for quarrelling. I have made up my mind to go. I will go. It is not a rash impulse. It is a decision taken silently and calmly. Let me pass."

He tried to clear the door. She pushed him back, suddenly seized with an energy which became all the fiercer as she felt her husband to be more inflexible. She had only a few minutes; and that was what frightened her. In those few minutes, by means of phrases, poor phrases flung out at random, she had to win the battle and to win it against a foe with whose mettle and obstinacy she was well acquainted.

"Let me pass," he repeated.

"Well, then, no, no, no!" she cried. "You shall not desert! No, you shall not do that infamous thing! There are things that one can't do. . . . This thing, Philippe, is monstrous! . . . Listen, Philippe, listen while I tell you. . . ."

She went up to him and, under her breath:

"Listen, Philippe . . . listen to this confession. . . . Philippe, you know what you did on Sunday, your cruelty to your father, to Suzanne, to all of us: well, yes, I understood it. . . . I suffered the pangs of death, I suffered more than any of the others. . . . Each word that you spoke burnt into me like fire. . . . But, all the same, Philippe, I understood. . . . You had to sacrifice us to the cause of peace. It was your right, it was your duty to victimize us all in order that you might save a whole nation. . . . But what you now propose to do. . . . Oh, the shame of it! . . . Listen, if you did that . . . I should think of you as one thinks of . . . I don't know what . . . as one thinks of the most contemptible, the most revolting . . ."

Shrugging his shoulders impatiently, he interrupted her:

"I can't help it if you do not understand. It is my right . . . and my duty also. . . ."

"Your duty is to join your regiment, now that war is declared, and to fight, yes, to fight for France, like every other Frenchman . . . like the first peasant that comes along, who may tremble with all his poor human flesh, it is true, and whose heart sinks within him and whose stomach turns cold, but who believes that his duty lies in being there . . . and who goes ahead, come what may! March on, as he does, Philippe! I have accepted all your opinions, I have shared them and backed them. . . . If there is to be an end of our union, at least let me address this last entreaty to you: join your regiment! . . . Your place is over there. . . ."

"My place is anywhere except where men commit the odious act of killing," exclaimed Philippe, who had listened to her in spite of himself and who now suddenly collected himself. "My place is with my friends. They trust me and I trust them. They are the men whom I must join."

"Where? In Paris?"

"No. We swore, at the first signal, to meet at Zurich. From there, we shall issue a manifesto calling upon all the thinkers and all the men of independent views in Germany and France."

"But no one will answer your appeal!"

"Never mind! The appeal will have gone forth. The world will have heard the protest of a few free men, professors like myself, tutors, writers, men who reflect, men who act in accordance with their convictions, and not like animals led to the slaughter."

"You must defend your country," said Marthe, seeking to gain time, in the hope that something would come to her assistance.

"I must defend my ideas!" declared Philippe. "If my country chooses to commit an act of folly, that is no reason why I should follow her. What nonsense it is, these two great nations, the most civilized in the world, going to war because they can't agree about the arrest of a petty official, or because one of them wants to eat up Morocco and

the other is incensed at not being invited to the ban-
quet! And, for that, they are going to fly at each
other's throats, like wild beasts! To scatter mourn-
ing and misery on every side! No, I refuse to take
part in it! These hands, Marthe, these hands shall
not kill! I have brothers in Germany as well as
France. I have no enmity against them. I will
not kill them."

She pretended to listen to his arguments with attention, knowing that, in this way, she would detain
him a little longer. And she said:

"Ah, your German brothers, whether they feel
enmity or not, you may be sure that they will march
against France! Is not your love for her the
greater?"

"Yes, yes, I love her, but just for the very reason
that she is the most generous and noble of countries, that in her alone the idea of revolt against the
law of blood and war can take root and sprout and
blossom."

"You will be treated as a coward."

"To-day, perhaps . . . but, in ten years, in
twenty years, we shall be treated as heroes. Our
names will be quoted as the names of the benefac-
tors of humanity. And it will be France again
that shall have had that honour . . . through us!
Through me!"

" But your name will be reviled during your life-time."

" Reviled by those whom I despise, by those who have the cast of mind of that captain — though he's one of the best of them — who laughs and jokes when he is sent to certain death, he and his company."

Marthe answered indignantly:

" It's the laughter of a Frenchman, Philippe, of a Frenchman hiding his anguish under a little light chaff. A glorious laughter, which forms the pride of our race! "

" One does not laugh in the presence of the death of others."

" Yes, Philippe, when it is to hide the danger from them and to keep all the horror and all the terror for one's self alone. . . . Listen, Philippe! . . ."

The sound of firing came from the distance, on the other side of the house. For some seconds, there was an uninterrupted crackle of musketry; then it came at rarer intervals; and, presently, there was no sound at all.

Marthe whispered:

" The first shot fired in the war, Philippe. . . . They are fighting on the frontier. . . . It's your country they are defending. . . . France is in dan-

ger. . . . Oh, doesn't your heart quiver like the
heart of a son? Don't you feel the wounds they
are giving her . . . the wounds they intend to give
her? . . ."

He wore his attitude of suffering, keeping his
arms crossed stiffly over his chest and half-closing
his eyes. He answered, sorrowfully:

"Yes, yes, I feel those wounds. . . . But why
is she fighting? For what mad love of glory? Is
she not intoxicated with successes and conquests?
Remember our journey through Europe. . . .
Wherever we went, we found traces of her passage:
cemeteries and charnel-houses to bear witness that
she was the great victress. Isn't that enough of conquests and triumphs?"

"But, fool that you are," cried Marthe, "she is
not trying to conquer! She is defending herself!
Picture this vision, for a moment: France invaded
once more . . . France dismembered . . . France
wiped from the face of the earth. . . ."

"But no, no," he said, with a gesture of protest,
"there is no question of that!"

"Yes, there is, there is a question of that: it's a
question of life or death to her. . . . And you, you
are deserting!"

Philippe did not stir. Marthe felt that he was,
if not shaken, at least anxious, uneasy. But, sud-

denly, he uncrossed his arms and, striking the table
with his fist:

" I must! I must! I promised to! . . . And I
was right to promise! And I will keep my oath!
What you call deserting is fighting, but fighting the
real fight! I too am going to wage war, but it will
be the war of independence and brains; and my
comrades in heroism are waiting for me. There,
Marthe, I won't listen to you any longer!"

She glued her back to the door, with her arms
outstretched:

" And the children! The children whom you are
abandoning!"

" You will send them to me later."

She raised her hand:

" Never, I swear it on their heads, never shall
you set eyes on them again! The sons of a deserter! . . . They will disown you!"

" They will love me, if they understand."

" I will teach them not to understand you."

" If they do not understand me, it is I who will
disown them. So much the worse for them!"

He took her by the shoulders and tried to push
her away. And, when Marthe resisted, he jostled her,
exasperated by the fear of the unforeseen obstacle
that might spring up, the arrival of his mother,
perhaps the apparition of old Morestal himself.

Marthe weakened. He at once seized her wrist
and pulled at the door. But, with one last effort, she
thrust back her husband and, panting, in despair:

"One word! One word more!" she implored.
"Listen, Philippe, don't do this thing. . . . And,
if you do not do it, well, I think I could . . . Oh,
it is horrible to coerce me like this! . . . Still, I
won't have you go. . . . Listen, Philippe. You
know my pride, the bitterness of my feelings and
all that I have suffered, all that I am suffering because of Suzanne. Well, I will forget everything.
I offer not only to forgive, but to forget. Never a
single word shall remind you of the past . . . never
an allusion . . . I swear it! But don't desert,
Philippe, I entreat you, don't do that!"

She hung on to his clothes and pressed herself
against him, stammering:

"No, don't do that. . . . Do not inflict that disgrace upon your children! The sons of a deserter!
. . . Oh, I entreat you, Philippe, stay! We will
go away together . . . and we will begin life again
as it was before. . . ."

She dragged herself at his feet, humble and sup-
plicating, and she received the terrible impression
that her words were of no avail. She was encoun-
tering a rival idea, against which all her strength
was shattered. Philippe did not hear her. No feeling of pity even turned him towards her.

Calmly, with an irresistible movement, he clasped Marthe's wrists, gathered them in one of his hands, opened the door with the other and, flinging his wife from him, fled.

Marthe was seized with a feeling akin to despair. However, the bag was still there and she believed that he would come back to fetch it. Then, realizing her mistake, she suddenly rose and started to run:

" Philippe! Philippe! " she cried.

Like him, she was thinking of some outside interference, of old Morestal, whom the outcries might attract and whom Philippe would find on his path.

" Philippe! Philippe! "

She became scared, not knowing where to look for him. There was nobody in the garden. She returned to the drawing-room, for she seemed to hear a sound of voices. And in fact she saw a sergeant and a private soldier hurriedly crossing the terrace, with the gardener's son leading the way.

" Follow me! " the brat commanded. " We'll go up to the roof. . . . You can see the whole valley from there. . . . Ah, the telescope! . . ."

He caught up the instrument as he passed.

Marthe rushed at them:

" What's happening? "

" Impossible to hold out over there," said the sergeant. " There are too many of them. . . . We're falling back. . . ."

" But, in that case, *they* will be coming? "

" Yes, yes, they're coming, right enough! . . ."

Marthe went out on the terrace. A swarm of soldiers came running up the staircase.

She saw Philippe in a corner. He was speaking to the men:

" Are they coming? "

" Yes."

" Have they crossed the frontier? "

" No, not yet."

He turned to his wife and said to her, as a piece of good news:

" They have not crossed the frontier yet."

And he went to meet another group of soldiers.

Then Marthe believed that fate had sent her the aid for which she was praying. She could now do nothing more but trust to events.

CHAPTER IV

THE SACRED SOIL

" BUGLER! . . . Sound the rally . . . at the double
. . . and quietly."

It was Captain Daspry who now arrived, with
a brisk gait, but with the grave and resolute face
of a leader who is commanding at a solemn moment.

He said to Philippe:

" Is M. Morestal still unwell? "

Mme. Morestal ran out from the house:

" My husband is asleep. . . . He is very tired.
. . . The morphia . . . But, if there is anything
you want, I can take his place. I know his intentions, his preparations."

" We shall attempt the impossible," said the officer. And, addressing his lieutenant, he added, " It
would have been madness to stay over there,
wouldn't it, Fabrègues? It's not a question of de-
molishing a few Uhlans, as we did, but of standing
our ground against a whole brigade who were
climbing the other slope. . . . Oh, it was all planned

long ago! . . . And M. Morestal is a jolly clever man! . . ."

The bugle sounded a low call and the Alpine Rifles emerged from every side, through the terrace, the garden and the back entrances.

"That will do!" said the officer to the bugler. "They have heard . . . and I don't want the enemy to hear as well."

He took out his watch:

"Twelve o'clock. . . . Two hours more, at least. . . . Oh, if I only had twenty-five minutes or half an hour in which to prepare my resistance. . . . But nothing will stop them. . . . The passage is free. . . ."

He called:

"Fabrègues!"

"Yes, captain."

"All the men in front of the coach-house, on the left of the garden. At the back of the coach-house is a hay-loft. Break down the door. . . ."

"Victor, show the gentleman the way," said Mme. Morestal to the servant. "Here is the key."

"In the loft," continued the captain, "you will find two hundred bags of plaster. . . . Use them to block up the parapet of this terrace. . . . Quick as you can! . . . Every minute is worth an hour."

He himself went to the parapet, measured it and counted the balusters. In the distance, within rifle-

range, the Col du Diable formed a deep gash between the great rocks.   Saboureux's Farm guarded
the entrance.   As yet, not a single figure of the
enemy showed.

"Ah, twenty minutes! . . . If I only had twenty
minutes!" repeated the officer.   "The position of
the Old Mill is hard to beat.   One would stand a
chance or two . . ."

An adjutant and a couple more soldiers appeared
at the top of the staircase.

"Well?" asked Captain Daspry.   "Are they
coming?"

"The vanguard was turning the corner of the
factory, at five hundred yards from the pass," replied the adjutant.

"Are there any more of our men behind you?"

"Yes, captain, there's Duvauchel.   He's
wounded.   They've laid him on a stretcher. . . ."

"Duvauchel!" cried the officer, anxiously.   "It's
not a serious wound, I hope?"

"Upon my word . . . I shouldn't like to say."

"Dash it all!   But then one saw nothing but that
devil in the front line. . . . There was no holding
him. . . ."

"Yes," chuckled the adjutant, "he has a way of
his own of deserting in the face of the enemy!
. . . He charges straight at them, the beggar!"

But Mme. Morestal grew frightened:

"A man wounded! I will go and prepare some bandages, get out the medicine-chest. . . . We have all that's wanted. . . . Will you come, Marthe?"

"Yes, mother," replied Marthe, without budging.

She did not remove her eyes from her husband and tried to read on Philippe's face the feelings that stirred him. She had first of all seen him go back to the drawing-room and cross the entrance-hall, as though he were thinking of the way out through the garden, which was still free. The sudden arrival of the riflemen pushed him back; and he talked to several of them in a low voice and gave them some bread and a flask of brandy. Then he returned to the terrace. His inaction, in the midst of the constant traffic to and fro, was obviously irksome to him. Twice he consulted the drawing-room clock; and Marthe guessed that he was thinking of the hour of the train and the time which he would need to reach Langoux Station. But she did not alarm herself. Every second was weaving bonds around him that tied him down without his knowing it; and it seemed to Marthe as though events had no other object than to make her husband's departure impossible.

The resistance, meanwhile, was being organized. Swiftly, the riflemen brought the bags of plaster,

which the captain at once ordered to be placed between every pair of balusters. Each of the bags
was of the height and width corresponding with
the dimensions of the intervals and left an empty
space, a loop-hole, on either side. And old Morestal had even had the forethought to match the
colour of the sacking with that of the parapet, so
that it might not be suspected in the distance that
there was a defence behind which sharpshooters lay
hidden.

On either side of the terrace, the wall surrounding
the garden was the object of similar cares. The
captain ordered the soldiers to set out bags at the
foot of the wall so as to make the top accessible
from the inside.

But a sound of shouting recalled the captain to
the drawing-room. The gardener's son came tumbling down from his observatory, yelling:

"Saboureux's Farm is on fire! You can see the
smoke! You can see the flames!"

The captain leapt out on the terrace.

The smoke was whirling above the barn. Gleams
kindled, faint as yet and hesitating. And, suddenly, as though set free, the flames shot up in
angry spirals. The wind at once beat them down
again. The roof of the house took fire. And, in
a few minutes, it was a violent flare, accompanied
by the quick blaze of the rotten beams, the dry

thatch, the trusses of hay and straw heaped up by the hundred in the barn and in the sheds.

" To work! " shouted the captain, gleefully. " The Col du Diable is blocked by the flames. . . . They'll last for quite fifteen or twenty minutes . . . and the enemy have no other road. . . ."

His excitement communicated itself to the men. Not one of them broke down beneath the weight of the bags, heavy though these were. The captain posted the non-commissioned officers at regular intervals, so that his orders could be passed on from the terrace to every end of the property.

Lieutenant Fabrègues came up. The materials were beginning to fall short and the lofty wall remained inaccessible to the marksmen in several places.

Mme. Morestal behaved like a heroine:

" Take the furniture, captain, the chairs, the tables. Break them up, if necessary. . . . Burn them even. . . . Do just as if my husband were here."

" M. Morestal said something about a stock of cartridges," asked the captain.

" In the boxes in the harness-room. Here are the keys."

The men redoubled their activity. The Old Mill was ransacked; and the soldiers passed laden with mattresses, sofas, old oak chests, hangings also and carpets, with which they stopped up the holes and the windows.

" The flames are spreading," said the captain, going to the top of the staircase. " There's nothing left of Farmer Saboureux's buildings. . . . But by what miracle . . . ? Who set the place on fire? . . ."

" I did."

A peasant stood at the top of the steps, in a scorched blouse, with his face all blackened.

" You, Saboureux? "

" Yes, I," growled Saboureux, fiercely. " I had to. . . . I heard you over there: ' If we could only stop them,' says you. ' If I had half an hour to spare!' . . . Well, there's your half an hour for you. . . . I set fire to the shanty."

" And very nearly roasted me inside it," grinned Old Poussière, who was with the farmer. " I was asleep in the straw. . . ."

The captain nodded his head:

" By Jove, Farmer Saboureux, but that's a damned sportsmanlike thing you've done! I formed a wrong opinion of you. I apologize. May I shake you by the hand? "

The peasant put out his hand and then walked away, with his back bent in two. He sat down in a corner of the drawing-room. Poussière also huddled into a chair, took a piece of bread from his

pocket, broke it and gave half to Saboureux, as
though he thought it only natural to share what he
had with the man who had nothing left.

"Here's Duvauchel, sir!" announced a rifleman.
"Here's Duvauchel!"

The staircase was too narrow and they had to
bring the stretcher round by the garden. The captain ran to meet the wounded man, who made an
effort to stand on his legs:

"What's up, Duvauchel? Are you hit?"

"Not I, sir, not I," said the man, whose face was
livid and his eyes burning with fever. "A cherry-
stone tickled my shoulder, by way of a lark. It's
nothing. . . ."

"But the blood's flowing. . . ."

"It's nothing, I tell you, sir. . . . I know all
about it. . . . Saw plenty of it as a greaser! . . .
It won't show in five minutes . . . and then I'm
off. . . ."

"Oh, of course, I forgot, you're deserting! . . ."

"Rather! The comrades are waiting for me.
. . ."

"Then begin by getting your wound dressed.
. . ."

"My wound dressed? Oh, that's a good one!
I tell you, sir, it's nothing . . . less than nothing
. . . a kiss . . . a puff of wind. . . ."

He stood up for an instant, but his eyelids flick-

ered, his hands sought for support and he fell back
upon the litter.

Mme. Morestal and Marthe hastened to his
side:

"Let me, mamma, please," said Marthe, "I'm
used to it. . . . But you've forgotten the absor-
bent wool . . . and the peroxide of hydrogen . . .
Quick, mamma . . . and more bandages, lots of
bandages. . . ."

Mme. Morestal went out. Marthe bent over the
wounded man and felt his pulse without delay:

"Quite right, it's nothing," she said. "The ar-
tery is uninjured."

She uncovered the wound and, very tenderly,
staunched the blood that trickled from it:

"The peroxide, quick, mamma."

She took the bottle which some one held out to
her and, raising her head, saw Suzanne stooping
like herself over the wounded man.

"M. Morestal is waking up," said the girl.
"Mme. Morestal sent me in her stead. . . ."

Marthe did not so much as start. She did not
even feel as though an unpleasant memory had
flitted through her mind, compelling her to make an
effort to suppress her hatred:

"Unroll the bandages," she said.

And Suzanne also was calm in the face of her
enemy. No sense of shame or embarrassment

troubled her. Their mingled breath caressed the soldier's face.

Nor did it seem that any memory of love existed between Philippe and Suzanne or that a carnal bond united them. They looked at each other unmoved. Marthe herself told Philippe to uncork a bottle of boracic. He did so. His hand touched Suzanne's. Neither he nor Suzanne felt a thrill.

Around them continued the uninterrupted work of the men, each of whom obeyed orders and executed them according to his own initiative, without fuss or confusion. The servants were all in the drawing-room. The women aided in the work. Amid the great anguish that oppressed every heart at the first formidable breath of war, no one thought of anything but his individual task, that contribution of heroism which fate was claiming from one and all. What mattered the petty wounds of pride, the petty griefs to which the subtleties of love give rise! What signified the petty treacheries of daily life!

"He's better," said Marthe. "Here, Suzanne, let him sniff at the smelling-salts."

Duvauchel opened his eyes. He saw Marthe and Suzanne, smiled and murmured:

"By Jingo! . . . It was worth while! . . . Duvauchel's a lucky dog! . . ."

But an unexpected silence fell upon the great drawing-room, like a spontaneous cessation of all the organs at work. And, suddenly, a voice was heard on the threshold:

"*They* have crossed the frontier! Two of them have crossed the frontier!"

And Victor exclaimed:

"And there are more coming! You can see their helmets. . . . They are coming! They are in France!"

The women fell on their knees. One of them moaned:

"O God, have pity on us!"

Marthe had joined Philippe at the terrace-door and they heard Captain Daspry repeating in a low voice, with an accent of despair:

"Yes, they are in France . . . they have crossed the frontier."

"They are in France, Philippe," said Marthe, taking her husband's hand.

And she felt his hand tremble.

Drawing himself up quickly, the captain commanded:

"Not a shot! . . . Let no one show himself!"

The order flew from mouth to mouth and silence and immobility reigned in the Old Mill, from one end to the other of the house and grounds. Each one stood at his post. All along the wall, the soldiers kept themselves hidden, perched upright on their improvised talus.

At that moment, one of the drawing-room doors opened and old Morestal appeared on his wife's arm. Dressed in a pair of trousers and a waistcoat, bare-headed, tangle-haired, with a handkerchief fastened round his neck, he staggered on his wavering legs. Nevertheless, a sort of gladness, like an inward smile, lighted his features.

"Let me be," he said to his wife, who was endeavouring to support him.

He steadied his gait and walked to the gun-rack, where the twelve rifles stood in a row.

He took out one with feverish haste, felt it, with the touch of a sportsman recognizing his favourite weapon, passed in front of Philippe, without appearing to see him, and went out on the terrace.

"You, M. Morestal!" said Captain Daspry.

Pointing to the frontier, the old man asked:

"Are they there?"

"Yes."

"Are you making a resistance?"

"Yes."

"Are there many of them?"

"There are twenty to one."

"If so . . . ?"

"We've got to."

" But . . ."

" We've got to, M. Morestal; and be easy, we shall stand our ground. . . . I'm certain of it."

Morestal said, in a low voice:

" Remember what I told you, captain. . . . The road is undermined at two hundred yards from the terrace. . . . A match and . . ."

" Oh," protested the officer, " I hope it won't come to that! I am expecting relief."

" Very well!" said Morestal. " But anything rather than let them come up to the Old Mill!"

" They won't come up. It's out of the question that they should come up before the arrival of the French troops."

" Good! As long as the Old Mill remains in our hands, they won't be able to man the heights and threaten Saint-Élophe."

They could plainly see columns of infantry winding along the Col du Diable. There, they divided and one part of the men turned towards the Butte-aux-Loups, while the others — consisting of the greater number, for this was evidently the enemy's object — went down towards the Étang-des Moines, to seize the high-road.

These disappeared for a moment, hidden by the bend of the ground.

The captain said to Morestal:

" Once the road is held and the assault begins, it

will be impossible to get away. . . . It would be better, therefore, for the ladies . . . and for you yourself . . ."

Morestal gave him such a look that the officer did not insist:

"Come, come," he said, smiling, "don't be angry. . . . Rather help me to make these good people understand. . . ."

He turned to the servants, to Victor, who was taking down a rifle, to the gardener, to Henriot, and warned them that none but combatants must stay at the Old Mill, as any man captured with arms in his hands exposed himself to reprisals.

They let him talk; and Victor, without thinking of retiring, answered:

"That's as may be, captain. But it's one of the things one doesn't think about. I'm staying."

"And you, Farmer Saboureux? You're running a big risk, if they prove that you set fire to your farm."

"I'm staying," growled the peasant, laconically.

"And you, tramp?"

Old Poussière had not finished eating the piece of bread which he had taken from his wallet. He was listening and observing, with eyes wide open and an evident effort to attend. He examined the captain, his uniform, the braid upon his sleeve, seemed to reflect on mysterious things, stood up and seized a rifle.

"That's right, Poussière," grinned Morestal. "You know your country right enough, once it needs defending."

A man had made the same movement as the tramp, almost at the same time. One more division in the gun-rack was empty.

It was Duvauchel, still rather unsteady on his pins, but wearing an undaunted look.

"What, Duvauchel!" asked Captain Daspry. "Aren't we deserting?"

"You're getting at me, captain! Let the beggars clear out of France first! I'll desert afterwards."

"But you've only one arm that's any good."

"A greaser's arm, captain . . . and a French greaser's at that . . . is worth two, any day."

"Pass me one of them rifles," said the gardener's son. "I know my way about with 'em."

Duvauchel began to laugh:

"You too, sonnie? You want one? You'll see, the babes at the breast will be rising up next, like the others. Lord, but it makes my blood boil to think that they're in France!"

All followed the captain, who allotted them a post along the parapet. The women busied themselves in placing ammunition within reach of the marksmen.

Marthe was left alone with her husband. She saw that the scene had stirred him. In the way in which those decent folk realized their duty and performed it without being compelled to, simply and spontaneously, there was that sort of greatness which touches a man to the very depths of his soul.

She said to him:

" Well, Philippe? "

His face was drawn; he did not reply.

She continued:

" Well, go. . . . What are you waiting for? No one will notice your flight. . . . Be quick. . . . Take the opportunity while it's here. . . ."

They heard the captain addressing his lieutenant:

" Keep down your head, Fabrègues, can't you? They'll see you, if you're not careful. . . ."

Marthe seized Philippe's arm and, bending towards him:

" Now confess that you can't go . . . that all this upsets your notions . . . and that your duty is here . . . that you feel it."

" There they are! There they are! " said a voice.

" Yes," said Captain Daspry, searching the road

through the orifice of a loop-hole, " yes, there they are! . . . At six hundred yards, at most . . . It's the vanguard. . . . They are skirting the pool and they haven't a notion that . . ."

A sergeant came to tell him that the enemy had hoisted a gun on the slope of the pass. The officer was alarmed, but old Morestal began to laugh:

" Let them bring up as many guns as they please! . . . They can only take up positions which we command and which I have noted. A few good marksmen are enough to keep them from placing a battery."

And, turning to his son, he said to him, quite naturally, as though nothing had ever parted them:

" Are you coming, Philippe? We'll demolish them between us."

Captain Daspry interfered:

" Don't fire! We are not discovered yet. Wait till I give the order. . . . There'll be time enough later. . . ."

Old Morestal had moved away.

Philippe walked resolutely towards the gate that led to the garden, to the open country. But he had not taken ten steps, when he stopped. He seemed to be vaguely suffering; and Marthe, who had not left his side, Marthe, anxious, full of mingled hope and apprehension, watched every phase of the tragic struggle:

" All the past is calling on you, Philippe; all the love for France that the past has bequeathed to you. Listen to its voice."

And, replying to every possible objection:

" Yes, I know, your intelligence rebels against it. But is one's intelligence everything? . . . Obey your instinct, Philippe. . . . It's your instinct that is right."

" No, no," he stammered, " one's instinct is never right. . . ."

" It is right. But for that, you would be far away by now. But you can't go. Your whole being refuses to go. Your legs have not the strength for flight."

The Col du Diable was pouring forth troops and more troops, whose swarming masses showed along the slope. Others must be coming by the Albern Road; and, on every side, along every path and through every gap, the men of Germany were invading the soil of France.

The vanguard reached the high-road, at the end of the Étang-des-Moines.

There was a dull roll of the drum; and, suddenly, in the near silence, a hoarse voice barked out a German word of command.

Philippe started as though he had been struck.

And Marthe clung to him, pitilessly:

" Do you hear, Philippe? Do you understand?

The German speech on French soil! Their language forced upon us!"

"Oh, no!" he said. "That can't be. . . . That will never be!"

"Why should it never be? Invasion comes first . . . and then conquest . . . and subjection. . . ."

Near them, the captain ordered:

"Let no one stir!"

Bullets spluttered against the walls, while the sounds of firing reverberated. A window-pane was smashed on the floor above. And more bullets broke fragments of stone from the coping of the parapet. The enemy, surprised at the disappearance of the French troops, were feeling their way before passing below that house, whose gloomy aspect must needs strike them as suspicious.

"Ah!" said a soldier, spinning on his heels and falling on the threshold of the drawing-room, his face covered with blood.

The women ran to his assistance.

Philippe gazed haggard-eyed at that man who was about to die, at that man who belonged to the same race, who lived under the same sky as himself, who breathed the same air, ate the same bread and drank the same wine.

Marthe had taken down a rifle and handed it to Philippe. He grasped it with a sort of despair:

"Who would ever have told me . . . ?" he stammered.

"I, Philippe . . . I was sure of you. We have not to do with theories, but with implacable facts. These are realities, to-day. . . . The enemy is treading the bit of earth where you were born, where you played as a child. The enemy is forcing his way into France. Defend her, Philippe. . . ."

He clenched his fists around his rifle and she saw that his eyes were full of tears.

He murmured, quivering with inward rebellion:

"Our sons will refuse . . . I shall teach them to refuse. . . . What I cannot do, what I have not the courage to do they shall do."

"Perhaps, but what does the future matter!" she said, eagerly. "What does to-morrow's duty matter! Our duty, yours and mine, is the duty of to-day."

A voice whispered:

"They're coming near, captain. . . . They're coming near. . . ."

Another voice, beside Philippe, the voice of one of the women tending the wounded man, moaned:

"He's dead. . . . Poor fellow! . . . He's dead. . . ."

The guns roared on the frontier.

"Are you coming, Philippe?" asked old Morestal.

" I'm coming, father," he said.

Very quickly, he walked out on the terrace and knelt beside his father, against the balusters. Marthe knelt down behind him and wept at the thought of what he must be suffering. Nevertheless, she did not doubt but that, notwithstanding his despair, he was acting in all conscience.

The captain said, clearly, and the order was repeated to the end of the garden:

" Fire as you please. . . . Sight at three hundred yards. . . ."

There were a few seconds of solemn waiting . . . then the terrible word:

" Fire! "

Yonder, along the barrel of his rifle, near an old oak in whose branches he once used to climb, Philippe saw a great lubber in uniform throw up his hands, bend his legs one after the other and stretch himself along the ground, slowly, as though to sleep. . . .

THE END

www.ingramcontent.com/pod-product-compliance
Lightning Source LLC
Chambersburg PA
CBHW021952010726
47494CB00003B/697